STRIKER

SUDDEN DEATH

NICK HALE

STRIKER

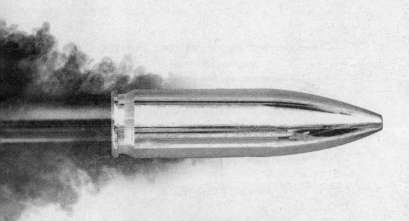

SUDDEN DEATH

NICK HALE

EGMONT

Special thanks to Michael Ford

To Paul, Allan and Richard – thanks for the inspiration

EGMONT
We bring stories to life

Striker: Sudden Death first published in Great Britain 2010
by Egmont UK Limited
239 Kensington High Street, London W8 6SA

Text copyright © Working Partners Ltd 2010
Cover design: Tom Hartley

The moral rights of the author have been asserted

ISBN 978 1 4052 4950 8

1 3 5 7 9 10 8 6 4 2

A CIP catalogue record for this title is available
from the British Library

Typeset by Avon DataSet Ltd, Bidford on Avon, Warwickshire
Printed and bound in Great Britain by the CPI Group

1

Jake sucked in a breath through his teeth as swirls of his blood circled the shower drain.

Olly Price's studs had left a six-inch gash down his right calf. The cut was probably deep enough to need stitches. Price had stood over him with a look of innocence, but Jake knew the tackle was no accident.

Worse though were the referee's words that still echoed in his head.

Your father would be ashamed of you, Jake. Go and get changed.

Jake showered quickly then stepped out into the changing room. A chill crept over his wet skin.

I shouldn't have punched him, he told himself. *Even if he did deserve it*.

The challenge had been high and dangerous. A fraction higher and Price would have gone right into Jake's knee. Then there would have been all sorts of trouble: snapped tendons, torn ligaments – 'a career-ender', that's what they called it.

And Jake knew well enough about those. He'd watched the tackle that ended his dad's playing days a hundred times. Munich, 1988. Steve Bastin lying on the pitch in agony, surrounded by his England team-mates. Twenty years later, his dad still walked with a slight limp.

Jake towelled himself dry and taped up his wound as best he could. He dressed in his school uniform, thankfully for the last time. Summer was starting. If he never saw Olly Price's smug face again, it would be too soon. The tension between them had been building ever since Jake had been transferred from an international school in Paris and had taken over the team captaincy in a matter of weeks.

Jake checked his watch. Half past five. He wasn't due to meet his dad for dinner until six-thirty, but it wouldn't hurt to get there early. He caught the Tube from Camden Town towards the West End, changing at Leicester Square for the Piccadilly Line. He decided to walk from Knightsbridge Station to use up a few more minutes. His leg hurt with every step.

Jake had already decided not to tell his dad about the red card – it would only mean the usual lecture:

What good are you to your team if you're back in the dressing room? When will you learn to control your temper?

Having Steve Bastin – or 'football legend Steve Bastin', as the papers insisted on calling him – as a dad could be a curse

2

as much as a blessing. Even though his dad had proved himself as a coach since his injury, he'd always be remembered as a great defender. Slow and steady. He didn't have the striker's instinct. You needed a bit of a temper, a bit of flair, to play up front. At least Jake thought so. But his mum disagreed, and six months ago she'd enrolled him on a course of boxing lessons – to 'channel his anger'.

He almost laughed to himself as he remembered the blood spurting from Price's nostrils. Those boxing lessons paid off!

But he was finished with boxing lessons and Olly Price – at least for the summer.

Traffic was heavy on Brompton Road and Jake noticed a cyclist up ahead weaving his way through the oncoming cars. Jake waited to cross the road with two parents and their young daughter. The man and woman were arguing about something. It reminded Jake of his own parents before their divorce: clipped comments under their breath and a refusal to look each other in the eye.

A black cab stopped a few metres away, and the passenger door suddenly opened. The cyclist didn't have time to stop, and swerved up on the pavement, shouting a curse. He didn't see the little girl in his path, but Jake did. Jake sprang forward, scooped her under the arms and twisted out of the way as the cyclist swished past.

'Olivia!' screamed her mother.

Jake released the little girl and she looked up at him with a mixture of surprise and curiosity. Her dad took her hand and pulled her towards him. 'Olivia, are you OK?'

The girl nodded without taking her eyes off Jake. He smiled at her, his heart still pumping from the near miss. He wished he could save her from the other hurt that was sure to follow when her parents stopped fighting and found lawyers.

The mother spoke to Jake: 'Thank you so much.'

'No problem,' Jake replied.

The dad rolled his eyes. 'You know what kids are like.'

I know what parents *are like*, Jake thought.

It was six-fifteen when Jake reached the restaurant where he had arranged to meet his dad. From the outside, Obed looked like an embassy, with its lightly tinted windows and the maîtres d'-cum-bouncers standing on either side of the door. Jake peered at the discreetly mounted menu and then looked through the glass to survey the interior. Circular tables, white tablecloths and low lighting. A bar occupied the rear, with double doors to the kitchens and a corridor to the toilets. The crowd was mostly business people coming in after work, faceless suits conferring over expensive dishes and fine wine.

And there at a corner table was his dad. He wasn't alone.

Another man sat opposite. Bald, but not much over forty, wearing an open-necked blue shirt. A scruffy waiter with a couple of days' worth of stubble laid a bowl of soup in front of the stranger, who draped his napkin across his lap. When the waiter had gone, his dad's guest leant across the table and said something with a grin, at which Jake's dad burst out laughing.

Jake felt a pang of frustration. His dad hadn't mentioned that they'd have company. He walked towards the entrance.

'Do you have reservation?' asked one of the giants guarding the door. He spoke in a thick Russian accent.

Jake might have been wearing his school uniform, but he wasn't going to let himself be intimidated. 'I'm meeting my dad,' he said. 'He's inside waiting for me.'

The doormen shared a look. The one who hadn't spoken nodded.

'Welcome to Obed, sir.'

He held open the door and Jake entered. His dad saw him straightaway and his face broke into a wide smile. He beckoned Jake over to the table.

'Andy,' his dad said to his companion, who was slowly sipping his soup. 'I want you to meet my son, Jake.' He turned to Jake. 'Jake, this is Andrew Chernoff. He's a talent scout.'

Jake's feelings of frustration evaporated. He'd met scouts

5

before; they sometimes came to games in the Sunday leagues or college matches and stood on the sidelines in their fancy suits, taking notes. Jake longed for his name to be one of those scribbled down; dreamt about a call-up to the reserves of one of the big sides.

'Hi, Mr Chernoff,' he said, smiling warmly and holding out his hand.

Andrew Chernoff took it with a firm handshake. His skin was like warm leather. He had a deep tan and Jake could tell he looked after himself by the way he moved. The lines around Chernoff's eyes crinkled as he smiled back at Jake. 'You look like your dad,' he said. His voice was soft, his accent Russian.

Jake was always being told that; he couldn't see it himself. True, his dad still had a full head of hair, greying though it was, and like Jake's it became wavy if he let it grow too long. And they both had blue eyes. But that was where the similarities ended. Jake was taller than his dad. Six foot one, and still growing. His dad had at least two stone of extra weight, though none of it was fat. He was built like a rock, while Jake was leaner. And Jake was quicker too, even if his dad hadn't had a limp.

'Don't embarrass the boy, Andy,' said Jake's dad.

Jake scowled. He hated being called a boy.

The unkempt waiter arrived back with some sort of stew for his dad. 'Would your son like anything to eat, sir?'

Jake wanted to snap that he could order for himself, but he swallowed back the words. 'I'll have *Kotmis Satsivi,* please,' said Jake. 'And a Coke.'

The waiter looked at him blankly – he was obviously stunned that an English boy knew the Russian for 'chicken with walnuts'. Jake had seen the dish on the menu outside. He'd had it a few times at his Russian friend Mika's house. It was Mika's mother's speciality.

'Very good, sir,' the waiter said, blinking, and disappeared towards the kitchen.

'So, who do you scout for?' Jake asked Chernoff. He tried to sound casual.

Jake's dad chuckled. 'I told you he was keen, Andy.'

Chernoff lowered his soup spoon and said, 'I used to work for a club in Spain, but I'm employed by Igor Popov now.'

Jake hadn't heard the name, but he didn't want to admit it.

'He's just set up a new club: the St Petersburg Tigers . . .' Chernoff's eyes flicked anxiously to Jake's dad as he tailed off.

Jake suddenly felt like the last person in the room to get the joke. He smiled unsurely. 'What's going on, Dad?'

Chernoff put a hand to his mouth and gave a sharp cough. 'Excuse me a moment . . .'

He scraped back his chair and walked hurriedly in the direction of the toilets.

'Tell me, how was football practice?' Jake's dad asked.

'Fine,' Jake replied. 'I scored.'

'You always do. And did you win?'

'Yes,' Jake lied. He didn't know the final score. 'What's wrong with Mr Chernoff? He seemed like he was in a hurry to get away.'

Jake's dad fiddled with his cutlery. 'He must have had something caught in his throat, I guess.'

Jake could tell he wasn't getting the full story. He knew that plenty of dodgy deals went on behind the scenes in football: secret meetings with agents, players being 'tapped up', but he didn't think his dad would be involved in all that.

'Why are you even meeting him?'

Jake's dad took a sip of water and looked at Jake seriously.

'There's something I have to tell you. Igor Popov . . . he's offered me a job: head coach of his new team.'

It took Jake a moment to process this.

'You mean we're going to Russia? That's great. I *love* Russia. I mean, I've just started at a new school, but, y'know, changing school again is no big deal.' *No more Olly Price*, he thought. 'What about the apartment?'

His dad held up a hand. 'Jake . . . I can't take you with me.'

Jake felt like he'd been punched in the gut. 'What are you talking about? Of course you can.'

'I'm sorry, Jake. Not this time.'

There was no room for negotiation in his dad's voice. Jake balled his fist under the table. The waiter returned and clumsily set down Jake's walnut chicken; a little of the sauce splashed over the rim of the plate. Jake waited until he'd gone.

'I've just come to London,' he hissed. 'To live with *you*.'

'I know that, Jake,' said his dad. 'With your mother travelling all over the place doing her photography it seemed the best idea.'

'Not that I had any say in it.'

His dad leant forward. 'Jake, listen . . .' His voice tailed off as Chernoff emerged from the toilet door and made his way back to the table. He looked a little unsteady on his feet and his skin appeared paler.

Jake's dad didn't seem to notice, and absently stirred his stew.

'Mr Chernoff, are you OK?' Jake asked.

'I'm fine . . . I think.' Chernoff took his seat.

The three of them sat in silence. The sound of their cutlery against the plates was deafening to Jake's ears as he chewed his chicken, trying to keep his temper from erupting again.

'There are some good Russian restaurants in Paris,' Jake's dad said. 'Did you go to many, Jake?'

'A couple,' Jake replied coldly.

The silence resumed. Chernoff kept taking nervous sips of water.

Jake ate until he could stand it no longer. He didn't care if they had company. 'Were you even planning to tell me?' he asked.

Jake's dad paused with his fork in front of his mouth, then laid it on his plate again. 'Of course. The offer only came up . . . today.'

Now Jake understood: the offer had come from Chernoff. He looked across at him. Chernoff's face was flushed. He was fiddling with his collar, as though he was too hot. Jake's warm feelings for his new acquaintance disappeared, scout or not.

'Maybe I should leave you two alone?' Chernoff said in a slightly rasping voice. He coughed again.

'Don't worry, you do what you have to,' Jake said to his dad. *Football first, everything and everyone else second*.

But his dad wasn't paying attention. He was leaning across the table towards Chernoff. 'Andy?' he said. 'Are you all right?'

Chernoff's fingers were tugging at the neck of his shirt.

His eyes were wide with panic. Jake instinctively pushed back his chair as Chernoff's face went from scarlet to purple. The veins across his temples stood out like worms under his skin. He tried to stand but his knees caught the underside of the table and he fell back in his seat, which threatened to topple over. A choking gurgle emerged from his mouth and saliva bubbled over his lower lip and chin.

Jake looked to his dad in horror. 'What's happening?'

Chernoff suddenly pitched forward, his face slamming into his soup. The brown liquid cascaded over the edge of the bowl as Chernoff rolled out of his seat and crumpled to the floor.

'Jesus, Andy!' Jake's dad jumped from his seat and rushed to help his friend.

Soup dripped from Chernoff's motionless face on to Jake's shoe. He pulled it back, stunned and revolted at the same time.

There was no doubt in Jake's mind that the Russian man was dead.

2

Jake's dad knelt at Chernoff's side. He placed both hands over the scout's chest and began pumping up and down. Jake flipped open his phone and dialled. 'Emergency,' said a calm voice in Jake's ear, 'which service do you require?'

'Ambulance, Obed restaurant, Brompton Road,' said Jake. 'A man's having a . . . he's dying . . . I think.'

Jake had just finished the call when the manager rushed over. 'What? How?' he stammered, looking from Chernoff to Jake.

'Just stand back,' Jake said, pushing at the crowd that had gathered. His dad continued CPR. For some reason, he wasn't breathing into Chernoff's mouth. Every so often he placed an ear to Chernoff's chest.

'Dad,' Jake said, 'you should give two breaths for ten compressions.'

His dad ignored him and continued compressions. He was still going, five minutes later, when Jake heard the distant wail of emergency sirens. The sound grew closer until an ambulance screeched to a halt outside. Strobes of blue light flashed across the restaurant interior.

Two paramedics carrying small holdalls burst into the dining area. One knelt beside Chernoff, her fingers feeling for a pulse on his neck. Jake's dad sat back, his head glistening with sweat.

'What's his name?' asked the paramedic matter-of-factly.

'It's Andrew,' said his dad quietly. 'Andrew Chernoff. I've checked his airways − they're clear.'

The woman put her ear to Chernoff's chest, with her fingers still at his throat. After a few seconds she straightened and gave a small shake of her head to her male colleague. Chernoff's lips were blue and his open eyes were unseeing.

The other customers were standing huddled like statues, but Jake caught a flash of movement by their table. The untidy waiter deftly picked up the bowl containing the remains of Chernoff's soup and his dirty napkin, then headed towards the kitchens.

Why is he clearing up now? Jake wondered.

As the ambulance crew lifted Chernoff on to a concertina stretcher, Jake slipped through the spectators, tracking the waiter. He peered through the small glass panels in the double-doors to the kitchen. He saw the waiter drop the napkin on a draining board beside an industrial dishwasher, then pick up Chernoff's bowl and place it in the sink. He turned on both taps, blasting it with water. Something about his calm, studied actions made Jake very uneasy.

He pushed open the doors and stepped in. 'What are you doing?'

The waiter was side-on to Jake. Jake's skin prickled. His brain said, *Run!*

But his feet didn't move . . .

'I said, what are you doing?' Jake repeated. His heart was pounding and it took a huge effort to keep his voice from trembling.

Suddenly the waiter's hand jerked up, spraying soap suds towards Jake. Jake ducked automatically, glimpsing a flash of metal. Something whooshed past his ear and thudded into the wall behind him. A meat cleaver was embedded in the doorframe, quivering.

Jake didn't stop to think – he ran straight at the waiter.

The waiter tried to kick out but Jake caught his foot and reached for the man's other leg, sweeping it away. They crashed together on to the lino floor, and Jake used all his upper body weight to pin the waiter down. The man said something in Russian, then tried to punch Jake in the side of the head. Jake reacted quickly and took the blow on his elbow, then he crunched his own fist into the Russian's teeth. Blood spattered around his mouth.

The waiter wouldn't give up. He jerked his hips and Jake toppled off him, his fingers catching the edge of the bin. Rubbish poured on top of him. He rolled over, fists up and ready to face his attacker.

But the Russian was disappearing out of a back door. Jake jumped up and went after him. He emerged into an alleyway. The waiter, shirt torn, was pelting towards Brompton Road. Jake sprinted in pursuit, but pain shot through his leg. He pulled up, grimacing. Warm blood was seeping through his trousers below the knee and he could feel the bandage he'd applied earlier hanging loose.

Jake limped out on to the busy street. He scanned left, then right, but the pavements were bustling with pedestrians carrying shopping bags and commuters walking home from work. The waiter was gone.

Jake kicked a bin angrily. He headed back down the alley, breathing heavily as he tried to swallow down his frustration. In the kitchen, the napkin was still on the draining board. Jake picked it up and hurried back through into the dining area. Everyone was outside now and he saw that the police had arrived as well: one patrol car and one unmarked vehicle − both silent, but with their blue lights slowly spinning. Jake's dad was leaning against the wall of the restaurant, rubbing his temples.

Jake dashed outside. 'Something's going on. Did you see the waiter? He tried to kill me. He –'

His dad grabbed him by the shoulders, scanned him up and down. 'Are you all right? Slow down, Jake. What happened?'

Jake took a breath and started again. 'The waiter attacked me,' he said slowly. 'He was throwing away Mr Chernoff's bowl. I got the napkin. I thought –'

His dad glanced back into the restaurant, then frowned at the napkin in Jake's hand. He took it, then pulled Jake tightly to him. 'You stupid boy. You could have been . . .' Jake twisted free of his dad's awkward embrace.

His dad's eyes were wet. Were there tears?

'Was . . . was Mr Chernoff murdered?' Jake asked.

But his dad was looking over Jake's shoulder and tucking Chernoff's soiled napkin into his jacket pocket. A suited man was making a beeline towards them. He nodded curtly to Jake's dad, flipping open his ID badge.

'Detective Farrimond, sir. The ambulance crew said you were dining with the deceased. I'm very sorry. Can I take your name, please?'

'Steve Bastin.'

Jake saw the flicker of recognition in the detective's face, and he was grateful the detective didn't pursue it.

'And you knew Andrew Chernoff, the victim, Mr Bastin?'

'Only professionally,' Jake's dad said.

What? thought Jake. *You were joking together like mates a quarter of an hour ago. You called him 'Andy'.*

'So you don't know if he was in poor health? Might this have been a heart attack?'

'It's possible,' Jake's dad said.

Jake couldn't believe the words coming out of his dad's mouth. Chernoff had looked in great shape.

'Do you know his next of kin?' the detective asked.

Jake's dad shook his head. 'He has a sister, I think. Lives in the States now. As I said, we weren't close.'

'Dad . . .' Jake began, but his dad silenced him with a hard stare.

The female paramedic came alongside the detective. 'We're going to head off now, if that's OK with you?'

'Excuse me a moment, sir,' said Detective Farrimond to Jake's dad.

As the detective and the paramedic separated themselves and talked in hushed tones, Jake turned to whisper, 'Dad, Mr Chernoff started getting ill when he was eating.'

His dad sighed, his eyes not leaving the detective and paramedic. 'It might have been a coincidence,' he said.

'But don't you think we should tell the police?' Jake noticed his dad's jaw tighten.

'Let the police do their job.' His dad frowned.

'What about the napkin? The waiter −'

Jake's dad spoke in a low but insistent tone. 'Jake, drop it . . . I'll handle this.'

The detective returned.

'Can we do anything else for you, detective?'

The investigator shook his head. 'No, sir. We'll notify the family.'

Jake's dad nodded. 'And you think it was cardiac arrest?'

'Almost certainly, sir. There'll be an autopsy; in cases like this it's procedure.'

Jake remembered the spittle and the gurgling sounds. He knew they weren't symptoms of a heart attack. And why wasn't his dad telling the police about the waiter?

A flash went off and Jake saw a photographer already on the scene, snapping pictures. When he lowered his camera, Jake noticed his wide-set pale eyes and square jaw. He had the kind of all-American look that Jake had come across so many times at his various international schools.

The 'American' was wearing a dark beanie hat, a strand of blond fringe peeking out above his brow. When he lifted his camera again, a uniformed policeman placed a sturdy arm in front of him and told him to move on.

The ambulance pulled away from the kerb, sirens and lights off. Detective Farrimond walked over and leant in close. 'I say, sir,' he said quietly, holding out his notepad. 'If you wouldn't mind . . . my son would be awfully grateful . . .'

Jake's dad gave a thin smile. 'Of course,' he said, taking the pad and pen. 'It's no problem. What's his name?'

'Er . . . it's Paul,' said the police officer.

Jake rolled his eyes. *Why do they always say it's for their sons? If this man has a son, he's probably never heard of Steve Bastin . . .*

'Thank you, sir,' said the detective, beaming as he took back the notepad. 'He'll be pleased as punch.'

Jake and his dad took a black cab home to Fulham in silence. The three-bedroom apartment they lived in was on two floors of a grand Victorian house set back from the road, with a semi-circular gravel drive out the front. The taxi skidded away, leaving them alone. When they reached the door, Jake's dad fished inside his wallet and took out a twenty-pound note.

'Are you still hungry? Why don't you order yourself a takeaway?' he said.

Jake took the money. 'Don't you want anything?'

Jake's dad shook his head. 'Lost my appetite.' He put his

hand on Jake's shoulder. 'Listen . . . I've got some work to do. We'll talk in the morning, OK?'

Jake tried to smile. It had been the same ever since he came to live in London: *in the morning, tomorrow, later . . .* He wondered, with Chernoff dead, would the move to Russia still happen? One look at his dad's drawn face told him now wasn't the time to ask. Even at sixteen, Jake was old enough to see something bigger was going on here. And he intended to get to the bottom of it, with or without his dad's help.

Up in his bedroom, Jake turned on his computer. The screen commands blinked into life and Jake's fingers shook over the keyboard as the full horror of the evening hit home. His stomach felt knotted up.

I saw someone die tonight.

It wasn't that he'd never seen a dead body. His mother was Irish Catholic and he remembered clearly the pale, waxy skin of his grandmother lying in her open coffin before the funeral in Dublin.

But this was different. This time Jake had watched life fade out of a man's eyes.

There was a voice chanting in his head, quiet but insistent: *I saw someone murdered.*

Jake logged on to the Internet and entered 'Andrew Chernoff' into the search engine. There were thousands of entries. The first was a profile of Chernoff from his playing days. He'd been a decent midfielder for Oxford United in the mid eighties, part of the team that took them to the old First Division. His stats were solid, averaging eight goals a season.

The profile said that he'd finished his playing days with Wrexham and that he'd retired in 1994, aged thirty-six. That made him fifty-two, much older than he'd looked. Like Jake's dad, he played in the days before big money made footballers into millionaires. Since quitting the pitch, Chernoff had made a name for himself as a top-flight scout, spotting gifted youngsters.

The second entry was from *The New York Times* and was dated only a week earlier. It was a piece about Chernoff's appointment to the St Petersburg Tigers. Apparently he was being paid handsomely to be the talent spotter for Igor Popov's new team, and had been given a blank cheque-book to travel the world in search of the very best players.

Jake's eyes were drawn further down the article to a subheading – 'Criminal Allegations' – where the journalist recounted rumours of wrongdoing within Igor Popov's oil empire:

Scandal continues to hound Popov, who made his fortune during the deregulation of the energy market following the

Soviet collapse. Accusations of fraud, protectionism and intimidation have long been associated with his business dealings, but the Russian government recently dropped its investigations.

With a fortune currently estimated at $18 billion, Popov is believed to be the seventh richest man in the world.

An image accompanying the article showed a smiling Chernoff standing on a training pitch with a short man in a sharp suit who was captioned as Popov. Jake stared closely at the face. There was no mistaking the rodent-like quality of Popov's thick dark hair and sharp eyes. It was wrong to judge, but perhaps there was some truth to the allegations . . .

Why would my dad want to work for a man like that?

The article had several links at the bottom, and one was a piece from the business pages: 'Igor Popov – Gangster or Opportunist?'

Jake clicked through. The article was by an American investigative journalist called Daniel Powell, whose picture accompanied the byline.

Jake's fingers clutched the mouse tighter.

It was the same man Jake had seen standing outside the Obed restaurant an hour before, taking photographs as

Chernoff's body was loaded into the back of the ambulance.

Jake swallowed and struggled to understand. *There was no way Powell could have reached the restaurant that quickly, unless . . .*

. . . unless he was already following Chernoff.

3

Jake woke to the sound of a phone ringing. It took him a moment to realise that he'd fallen asleep across the computer keyboard. The article about Popov was still on screen. The evening came flooding back: Chernoff's death. His dad's weird behaviour. He checked the clock; it was nearly midnight. The phone stopped abruptly.

Must have been a wrong number. Who'd ring at this time of night?

Jake's mouth was dry. He needed water. He got up and tiptoed out to the landing. The stairs were in darkness but he didn't switch the light on, opting to feel his way down. The sound of a muffled voice came from his dad's study, next to the kitchen. The study door was ajar. Jake stopped to listen.

'How quickly can the lab turn it around, Sam?' his dad asked.

The lab? Who's he speaking to?

'That's great,' he said. 'We can't afford to wait six weeks for the police to bungle their way through a tox analysis.'

Jake pushed the door open a fraction and peered through the crack. His dad was sitting at his desk, the phone to his ear as he pushed something with a pencil. Jake couldn't see what it was.

'I just can't believe Andy's been murdered.' A pause. 'I know, I know, I'm jumping to conclusions.'

His dad swung slightly in the chair and Jake saw what was on the desk. Chernoff's napkin, still stained with food.

After listening for a moment, his dad looked up towards the ceiling. 'I don't know,' he said. 'I'm not ready to take on another job. But someone's going to pay.' His dad paused then shook his head before responding. 'Jake's only just moved in. I can't up sticks and ship out – not with everything that's going on.' Another pause. 'You too, Sam. I'll be waiting.'

His dad hung up. He put the napkin into an envelope, sealed the top, and walked towards his bookcase. Jake fought the urge to scurry back upstairs.

His dad pulled out two books and placed them on the floor. Then two more.

What's he doing?

Soon there was a messy stack of twenty or so books.

25

His dad seemed to be inspecting the back of the shelf very carefully. Then a metal door swung open.

A safe! Jake had never known they had one. His dad knelt down and looked to be tying his shoelace. His foot was concealed behind the pile of books. When he straightened up, he was holding a gun.

Jake's breathing stopped. The gun must have been in an ankle holster. It had been there all night. All through dinner. All through the conversation with the detective.

Why does he have a gun?

Jake remembered his dad's words. *Another job. Someone's got to pay.*

My dad might be a killer.

Jake swallowed drily. It couldn't be true. Could it?

The doorbell chimed.

Jake darted from the door and ran up the stairs. He reached the middle step and turned as his dad emerged from the study. He was carrying the envelope.

'Oh!' he said. 'I thought you were in bed, Jake.'

'I heard the bell,' Jake replied, taking a few steps back down.

His dad got to the door first. On the step was a man dressed in leathers and wearing a helmet. In the street outside, under the driving rain, was a motorbike with its lights on. His dad handed the rider the envelope, nodded, and closed the door.

'Who was that?' Jake asked.

'Just a courier,' his dad said breezily. 'Player contract, y'know. Lawyers rest for no man. Sleep well, hey.'

A draught blew in from the door, making Jake shiver. His dad seemed like an actor, reading lines. How could he lie so easily? 'Sure,' Jake said, trying to control his voice. 'I'm just going to get a glass of water.'

As he filled his glass in the kitchen, he heard the door to the study click shut.

Could he trust anything his dad said any more?

An hour later, Jake was playing an online boxing game when he heard an engine outside. His first thought was *Police*. They'd probably run checks by now and realised his dad wasn't telling the truth earlier. Maybe they'd already found evidence linking him with Chernoff's death. Would they search the house? Find the gun in the safe? Traces of poison? Jake's mind reeled. He imagined his dad being led away in handcuffs. A part of him thought: *That's what you deserve*.

He went to the window. Outside, a sleek black Mercedes had pulled up. A man climbed out of the driver's seat and put up an umbrella. He opened the rear door for another man, obviously his boss. Together, they made their way towards the front door of the apartment. Jake left his bedroom and hopped down the stairs. The bell rang just before he got there. He opened the door immediately.

Jake recognised the man standing in the doorway straightaway. He was short and wiry, wearing a black dinner jacket and bow tie. His face had shifting, suspicious features. The face from the newspaper article.

Igor Popov.

Jake couldn't tell if it was the chill from outdoors, or something else. The temperature seemed to drop five degrees. Behind Popov, a shaven-headed, black-suited bodyguard the size of a bear was shaking the raindrops off the umbrella.

'This is Mr Bastin's residence?' said Popov in a heavy Russian accent.

'Who is it, Jake?' asked his dad. He was at the top of the stairs wearing his dressing gown.

'Steven!' said Popov, ignoring Jake and holding out both hands. 'Steven, I came as soon as I heard. I was at the opera in Covent Garden. I'm so dreadfully sorry about our friend. Andrew was a credit to football.'

With his hand on the banister, his dad descended as quickly as his limp would allow. He eased Jake aside and gestured with a sweeping hand. 'Please, come in, Mr Popov.'

There was something in his dad's tone that Jake

hadn't heard before. He sounded like a servant speaking to his master.

Popov seized Jake's dad's elbow in one hand and the other went round his back in a light embrace. When he pulled away, Jake thought he saw a mist in Popov's eyes. Whether it was genuine or not, he couldn't tell.

'Andrew was a good friend,' his dad said. 'And in good health. As far as I know.'

Jake stared at his dad. Now Chernoff was a good friend again! And 'in good health'!

'Yes, yes,' said Popov. 'A tragedy.' He pointed to Jake. 'And this must be your son. The likeness is unmistakeable.' Popov held out his hand to Jake. 'Igor Popov. Pleased to make your acquaintance.'

Jake stepped up and took the hand. 'Jake Bastin,' he said. 'You're the man who wants to take my dad to Russia.'

He spoke the words neutrally, but the smile on Popov's face slipped to half-mast for a second, then returned with a flash of white teeth. He looked past to Jake's dad.

'So Andrew told you of my offer before . . .' he paused. He looked at Jake again. 'Jake, I have a great respect for your dad. He was a phenomenal player, and he's a real statesman for the game −'

'Jake,' said his dad. 'I'd like to speak to Mr Popov alone.'

Jake was about to argue, but Popov spoke first.

'There's no need to send the boy away, Steven. How will he become a young man if he is always sent away when the men talk business? Let him stay, why not?'

Jake's dad pressed his lips together in a smile. 'As you wish, Mr Popov.' He gestured to the study. 'This way, please.'

The books were back on the shelf, but Jake couldn't forget what he'd seen earlier that night.

The bodyguard followed them into the room, then stood by the door. Jake couldn't help feeling that they were being caged in.

'Mr Popov,' his dad said. 'Let me get straight to the point. I'm not sure that I can accept your generous offer –'

Popov held up both palms and Jake's dad stopped speaking. 'Is it the money, Steven? If so, I can –'

'It's not the money,' his dad said. 'It's a personal matter. You see, my son and I have only just begun living together. Perhaps Andrew didn't tell you. Until recently Jake has lived with my ex-wife, or been at an international boarding school, but now I feel he needs a period of *stability*.'

He's using me, thought Jake. *He's scared and he's making excuses.*

'And now,' continued his dad, 'now Andrew's dead, well, I really think . . .'

Popov smiled widely, but there was no joy in his eyes. 'Of course, of course. You feel you must put your family first. But think what we could achieve together.' He let the words hang for a moment, before lowering his voice to a theatrical whisper. 'I have an admission to make, Steven. I was going to tell you this later, but now seems like a good time.'

'Yes?' Jake's dad asked.

'I have made a new signing. It's not announced to the press yet, because the deal is highly sensitive. Would you like to know who it is?'

Despite himself, Jake leant forward. The gleam in Popov's eye promised something really special, but surely no top player would go to a new, untried team. No matter what the money was.

His dad nodded slowly.

'Well,' said Popov, 'you know the rest of the team already, but I thought we were still missing a little something up front. Another striker. So I bought the best . . .' Popov paused, obviously relishing the moment. 'Devon Taylor.'

'Wha−?' interrupted Jake. 'How? Taylor's on a contract with Barcelona for another three years.' The transfer a year before had been huge news, the biggest ever signing.

Popov waved his hand and smiled at Jake. 'Contracts? They're not so important. The crucial thing is to have the right team.' Popov paused, then looked meaningfully at Jake's dad. 'And the right manager.'

His dad had kept his composure through Jake's outburst. 'Taylor is quite a coup,' he said. 'He's a brilliant young talent.'

'And of course we have the new stadium, funded by my American friend Christian Truman and his company, Truman Oil. State of the art technology, a capacity of eighty thousand. Leisure facilities that rival –'

'I've seen the plans, Mr Popov,' said Jake's dad. 'It's very impressive. But I have other concerns to factor in. Like my son.'

'And I respect them, Steven,' said Popov. 'Your son would of course be more than welcome to join you in St Petersburg. Wouldn't you like that, young man?'

'My son has a life here,' Jake's dad said quickly.

Typical, Jake thought. *Don't let me speak for myself.*

Jake noticed that the vein running down the centre of Popov's forehead was a little pronounced; blue under the Russian's pale skin.

'I think you have been – how do you say – *perturbed* by your friend's death, so I will leave you to your grief. Don't give me your answer about the coaching position now.' Popov took out a silver case from his jacket and opened it. He placed

32

a card on the bookshelf beside the door. 'This is my private number. Sleep on it.'

Popov nodded to the bodyguard, who opened the study door with one of his massive fists. The meeting was clearly over.

At the front door, Popov waited while his attendant opened the umbrella, then stepped underneath. The rain spattered off the top.

'I look forward to speaking with you again, Steven.'

Jake's dad smiled. 'I don't think I'm going to change my mind, but thank you for coming over.'

Jake and his dad watched as the Mercedes pulled away, then his dad closed the door.

'So are you going to take the job, or not?' Jake asked.

'I don't know yet,' his dad replied.

'Well, when will you know?' Jake said. He couldn't keep the anger out of his voice.

'Just go to bed, Jake. I'll see you tomorrow.'

Before Jake could answer, his dad was back in his study, shutting the door behind him.

In his room, Jake lay on his back on his bed, staring at the ceiling.

Maybe I should have stayed in Paris.

He had been nervous about coming back to London.

His dad had always been a footballer rather than a dad. They'd both tacitly understood that this was the chance to build a relationship. But it was like building a house of cards. A small wobble could bring down the whole thing.

4

'I'm making some eggs,' his dad said as Jake came into the kitchen next morning. 'You want some?'

As if everything's just normal, thought Jake.

'I'll get myself some fruit,' he replied stiffly.

His dad was facing the stove, fiddling with a pan. He was also wearing a shirt and tie. That was pretty weird for a Saturday. After years of early rises for away games, he normally liked to take it easy at the weekends.

Jake took a banana from the bowl and went to the French windows. The sun was glinting through a few thin shreds of cloud on to the small back garden. After last night's rain, the trees had that fresh, just-washed look. Jake's head, in contrast, felt overcast and his thoughts dulled. He'd hardly slept a wink.

He finished the banana. 'Have you decided what you're going to do?' Jake asked.

His dad stopped stirring his eggs for a second, then resumed. 'It's a good job, Jake,' he began. 'Good money, too –'

'So you're going to take it?' Jake interrupted.

His dad took the pan off the stove and looked at him. By the dark smudges under his eyes, Jake guessed he hadn't had the best night's sleep either.

He nodded. 'I am.'

Jake dropped the banana skin in the rubbish bin. 'And what do I do? Stay in London on my own?'

His dad's face hardened. 'No, you'll go to your mum's. In Milan.'

Just like that. No discussion, no compromise. Jake fought the urge to kick the bin across the room. He loved his mother, but when she wasn't off photographing models, she was at home, reviewing her work. Even Jake could get bored of staring at pictures of hot girls after a couple of hours.

'So you just ditch me?' he asked his dad. 'Sub me off like one of your players?'

The lines on his dad's face softened again. 'It's not like that, Jake, and you know it.'

'If you send me away now,' Jake said, 'I'll never forgive you.'

'You don't mean that,' his dad said. 'It's you that I'm worried about –'

But Jake didn't give him time to finish. 'Then prove it,' he said. 'Let me come to Russia.'

His dad took a deep breath. He brought both hands, palms together, in front of his mouth, as if in prayer, and stared into the distance. Thinking hard.

Almost there, thought Jake.

His dad lowered his hands, looked Jake dead in the eyes. 'OK, Jake,' he said. 'But only for a couple of weeks. On a trial basis.'

Jake smiled. 'Thanks, Dad. I won't get in the way, I promise.'

But his dad wasn't returning the smile. If anything, he looked graver than ever. 'I'll let your mother know,' he said with a sigh.

Russia isn't just about football, is it? Jake thought. He'd promised he wouldn't get in the way, but it wasn't a promise he intended to keep.

'Jake, do you really need three sets of shin-pads?' his dad asked. He was sitting on the floor taping up the last of the removal boxes.

Jake laughed. Since his dad had agreed to let him come to Russia the events at Obed and afterwards had slipped his mind from time to time. When the memories returned, they were like pressure on a forgotten bruise: painful, but temporary. His dad had been preoccupied with preparation, but they'd still found time for a couple of kick-abouts in the park.

Like a normal father and son.

Almost.

'You know what some of these defenders are like,' he said, punching his dad playfully on the shoulder. 'Real clumsy bruisers.'

'Watch it!' his dad replied. 'Remember, I'm your ticket to Russia.'

A removal man walked past, carrying a box reading POP23, the flight number of Igor Popov's private jet. His dad had already signed autographs for all the big movers. They'd gawped like schoolboys when they'd realised whose stuff they were shifting.

Popov had assured them that all their needs would be taken care of once they were in Russia, so Jake and his dad weren't taking much. It was mainly clothes, football gear and documents relating to the new job. The rest, all the furniture and their other possessions, would stay. His dad always kept a base in London.

Jake wondered if his dad had packed the gun, wrapped it inside a towel or something in the box marked 'Personal'.

Over the last few days, he'd found himself making excuses

for that. Maybe the gun was for self-defence. Maybe it wasn't even real – a replica, just for show. It didn't mean anything, did it? Lots of people had guns. Perhaps he'd let the shock of Chernoff's death get the better of him.

A ring on the doorbell, and Jake jumped over the edge of the couch to answer it. Standing, almost filling the doorframe, was the bodyguard who'd visited before with Igor Popov.

'You are ready,' he said. Not a question, not a statement. Somewhere in between.

'Just about,' said Jake. He called to his dad, 'Hey, Bruiser, the driver's here!'

The Russian grumbled something into a phone, and Jake sprinted upstairs to fetch his jacket and iPod.

This is it! he thought. *I'm going to Russia!*

It was late afternoon when Jake and his dad finally slipped into the sleek leather seat of Popov's limo. The bodyguard-cum-chauffeur closed the door behind them. The car's suspension dipped as the mountain of muscle parked himself in the driver's seat.

'Help yourself to refreshments,' he said, pointing a stubby finger to the compartment between the front seats.

The car started with a purr and eased out into the street. With the tinted windows, it was like being cocooned in a submarine. Jake popped the fridge door and took out a can of Red Bull. *This is travelling in style*, he thought.

He cracked the can with a hiss. 'You want anything, Dad?'

His dad gave a thin smile and shook his head. 'I'm good, thanks.'

Jake saw the button he assumed would wind down the window and pressed it. Instead, the headrest in front gave a beep. A cover lifted up to reveal a small monitor underneath.

'Cool!' said Jake. He hit the play button and the screen blinked into life.

It was a compilation of highlights from the previous La Liga season. It took Jake a second or two to realise the focus of the tape was none other than Devon Taylor. In one sequence he took a sixty-yard cross-field pass on his chest, then volleyed it another thirty into the top corner. The goalkeeper didn't even move. Jake rewound the video and watched it again.

One day, Jake promised himself.

'Will I meet Devon Taylor?' he asked.

His dad looked away from him, out of the window. 'I'm sure you will,' he said.

Jake had travelled first class in the past, but nothing compared with the treatment they received at Heathrow airport courtesy of Igor Popov. The limo was waved through an external security check, their passports given only the briefest glance.

The limo pulled up beside a small hangar where a Learjet was parked. It looked like a toy – pointed like a dart, with a row of six windows perched high on the fuselage. The wings looked impossibly narrow and flimsy, their points upturned at either end. The logo on the tail fin was the 'PI' of Popov Industries. The crate holding their belongings was already being loaded into the small cargo hold at the rear as Jake and his dad were ushered up the front steps.

A man wearing a peaked cap greeted them. Beside him stood a statuesque blonde woman with startling blue eyes. With her long legs and curves she wouldn't have looked out of place on the catwalk.

'I'm Max Siegel, your co-pilot for today,' said the man. 'And this is Helga. She'll be able to help you with anything you require during the flight. For now, please do take a seat – we should have clearance for take-off any minute.'

'Thank you,' said Jake's dad. Jake noticed Helga was smiling at his dad appreciatively. *Typical*, thought Jake. *Another fan*. The cockpit was blocked off with only a curtain, which was pulled to the side. Jake quickly surveyed the wall-mounted buttons and gauges and saw another man, presumably the captain, sitting in front of them. He was checking details on a computer display.

They followed Helga's swaying hips back through another

curtain. Her perfume was fragrant and rich – too rich. It made Jake cough and his eyes water. *Who needs that much perfume?*

The main compartment was nothing like the planes Jake had flown in before. There were no rows of cramped identical seats, no narrow aisle. Instead, there were plush sofas arranged around low tables, and huge reclining chairs. Proper light fittings with dimmer switches on the walls. At the far end was a marble bar with rows of bottles; further still, past another open curtain, was what looked like a kitchen.

A man sat with his back to them on one of the sofas, his Timberland boots on a footrest. Jake recognised the beanie hat at once. The man turned round, giving a wide pristine smile. 'You . . .' Jake mumbled.

The journalist from outside Obed. What was his name?

'Hi,' said the man, climbing out of his seat and extending his hand. 'Daniel Powell,' he said in a New York accent. 'I hope you don't mind sharing the plane with me.'

Jake couldn't speak. *What's he doing here?*

His dad took the outstretched hand. 'Not at all, Daniel. Mr Popov said we might have some company. This is my son, Jake.'

Jake managed to gather himself. 'Nice to meet you.'

Luckily, Helga interrupted them. 'If you could take your seats, gentlemen,' she said. 'We've been cleared for take-off.'

Jake kept sneaking glances at Daniel Powell as the Learjet taxied on to the runway, accelerated and lifted into the sky.

'What's he doing here?' he finally whispered to his dad.

'I forgot to tell you. Daniel Powell is doing a profile on the Tigers for an American sports magazine. We'll be seeing a lot more of him over the next couple of weeks.'

The captain informed them over the tannoy that they'd be airborne for approximately five hours. Jake's dad was asleep by the time they reached the Flemish coast, but Jake couldn't relax. He tried watching an action movie but the plot was dumb and he found concentrating difficult. The man who had written about Chernoff *and* Popov was sitting a few feet away. The man who had been outside the restaurant when Chernoff died.

Jake switched off the movie. His dad was snoring softly.

Time to do a little investigating. Powell knows something about Chernoff – I need to find out what.

He stood up and walked as casually as possible past Daniel Powell. He didn't need the loo, but it provided a convenient excuse. The journalist was tapping away on a slim Macintosh

43

laptop, and didn't look up. In the toilet, Jake worked out how he'd start a casual conversation with Powell.

But on Jake's way back it was Powell who spoke first. 'Why don't you take a seat, Jake?'

Jake did, easing himself on to a sofa. Powell leant back. 'You must be excited – this is a big move for your dad.'

Jake shrugged. 'Sure. Dad's coached big teams before, though.'

Powell nodded and gave a disarming smile. 'They say Igor Popov is the richest owner in the game.'

'Money doesn't always buy success,' Jake replied. 'You can have the most expensive players in the world, but without the right coach you won't win anything.'

Powell nodded. 'You seem to know your stuff.'

Jake wasn't falling for the compliment. He knew enough about journalists to know they couldn't be trusted. *Sharks*, his dad called them. One sniff of your blood and they'd happily write the story with it. But how could he move to the topic of Chernoff?

'Tell me,' continued Powell. 'Do you know when your father first met Mr Popov?'

The smile was still there, but something about Powell's posture had changed. Jake didn't like it. He was being played, when he wanted to be the player.

'No,' he said, 'I don't.'

'Jake,' said his dad sleepily from further up the cabin. 'Don't be bothering Mr Powell.'

Jake had missed his chance. With his dad awake and clearly eavesdropping, Jake couldn't swing the conversation to Chernoff. 'Excuse me,' Jake said to Powell.

'Of course,' said the American. 'Maybe we'll catch up another time.'

Jake left the journalist and sat down again across from his dad. His dad leant closer. 'I don't want you to talk to Daniel Powell,' he murmured.

'Why?' asked Jake.

'Journalists are always fishing for stories, new angles.' His dad waved his hand as though it wasn't important. 'And we don't need any bad publicity.' With that, he laid back and closed his eyes.

Jake studied his dad for a moment, as if he could somehow read the truth in the face that he, and the world, thought they knew so well.

As dusk drew over the sky, the land below had turned white, and Jake guessed they were cruising over southern Finland. St Petersburg was three hours ahead of London, so they'd be landing in the middle of the night.

Helga sashayed through with a tray holding two champagne flutes and an orange juice.

'A little bubbly before we land.' Helga nudged Jake's dad awake and forced one into his hand. 'And for you,' Helga said with a wide smile at Jake as she handed him the orange juice. Jake's eyes watered and he coughed as her over-powering perfume engulfed him.

'Thanks,' Powell said, snatching the other flute as she passed. 'Don't mind if I do.' He gulped it down.

'Cheers, everyone!' Helga said, raising an imaginary glass and returning to the front of the plane. Jake's dad set the glass on the table, turned over and went back to sleep.

At last Jake felt tired. He needed a pillow. He pressed the call button for the flight attendant. A few seconds passed and Helga came through. Her smiles from earlier had gone and her skin seemed even paler: glacial, like the landscape below.

'Could I have a pillow?' he asked.

She frowned. 'We'll be landing soon,' she said briskly.

'Oh,' said Jake. He checked his watch. At least another hour. 'Are you sure?'

'Of course I'm sure,' she said, before striding back towards the cockpit.

What's got into her? Jake wondered.

A minute later Helga came through again, carrying a small bag. Jake thought she must have changed her mind and brought him a pillow. But she strode by without a word, disappearing past Daniel Powell's seat and into the rear of the plane where the cargo was stored.

Jake tried to make himself comfortable on the sofa, lying sideways. He looked up at the curtain that separated the cockpit from the rest of the cabin. A dark dribble of liquid was forming a puddle beneath the curtain's edge.

One of the pilots must have spilt his coffee, Jake thought.

Jake picked up a napkin and walked over to wipe the floor. Only when he was close did he realise the liquid was a deep red. Definitely not coffee.

Jake pushed the curtain aside.

Max Siegel, the co-pilot, was slumped backward in his chair as though asleep. The small red hole in his forehead told a different story, as did the hole in the pilot's chest. His white shirt was soaked with blood, which trickled down his limp arm and on to the floor.

Both pilots had been shot.

5

'**D**ad! Wake up!' Jake ran back into the cabin and shook his dad's shoulders.

His dad's eyes snapped open. He gripped Jake's arms.

'What is it?' he shouted. 'What's wrong?'

'The pilots – they've been shot.'

His dad sprang to his feet, upsetting the champagne glass that rested on the table. 'What are you talking about?'

Jake dragged his dad into the aisle and pointed. He still couldn't believe what he was seeing. Two men. Murdered.

The co-pilot's body sagged gently to one side, then rolled forward on to the steering column. The plane's engines roared, the right wing jerking suddenly upward.

Jake was thrown sideways, crashing over another table and slamming his head against the fuselage wall. The bottles in the bar fell one by one, smashing across the marble surface, and showering the floor with glass.

His dad stumbled beside him and caught himself on the edge of a sofa. With one hand holding himself against the wall, he edged his way towards the cockpit. Jake followed, trying to avoid the growing pool of blood.

His dad heaved the co-pilot's body off the control panel and pushed it roughly out of the seat as though he saw dead bodies every day. Jake stepped forward, scanning the levers and gauges in panic. It may as well have been the *Starship Enterprise*. He recognised the odd word − *Anti-Ice*, *Lights*, *Pressurisation* − but the switches, buttons and dials were mostly marked with coded abbreviations.

We haven't got a chance.

The plane's nose was now tipping downward and to the left. Shreds of cloud ripped past the cockpit window.

'What do we do?' Jake asked, his throat tight with fear.

His dad grabbed the steering column and tugged it around. The plane's right side dipped sharply, as the wings rocked the other way. Jake fell against the dead pilot and cried out in disgust.

'Check Powell,' his dad said.

'But what about you?' Jake asked.

'Just do it!' shouted his dad. 'Now.'

Jake stumbled backward out of the cockpit. His dad reached across the panel and eased out a lever.

What's he doing? Jake thought. He knew his dad had had a couple of flying lessons in the 1980s, but this was crazy. He surely couldn't fly something like this.

Powell was in his seat, but slumped across the sofa, hidden by the backrest. At first, Jake assumed the worst. But there was no blood. As he tried to wake him, the journalist moaned groggily. It was as if he was drunk.

Or drugged. Jake remembered Helga's smiling face as she offered Powell a glass of champagne.

Helga. Had she killed the pilots? Drugged Powell? It was the only answer.

Jake left Powell in his seat and headed towards the back of the plane, past the remains of the bar, where the air was thick with the sharp smells of mingled spirits. His dad had finally managed to level the plane.

Past the toilet was a small kitchen area, all stainless steel and neat compartments. Beyond that, a hatch, swinging open. Jake climbed through the hatch on his hands and knees. This route was obviously meant for crew only.

The cargo hold took up almost the back third of the plane. A set of metal steps led down to telemetric equipment panels. The air was colder, like stepping into a refrigeration unit. Jake spotted some of the boxes they were bringing with them, stacked in place and secured with canvas webbing.

And beyond that was Helga.

She was bent over, changing her high-heels for some heavy-duty boots. On her back was a rucksack, secured tightly over her cabin-crew uniform.

A parachute.

'Stop!' Jake yelled.

Helga's head snapped round and she fixed him with her blue eyes.

Jake noticed a spatter of blood on her uniform. Her eyes dropped to the top of a crate between them. On it rested a gun.

They both lunged for the weapon, but she was closer.

As she reached the crate, the plane juddered through a pocket of turbulence. Her outstretched fingers caught the gun's hilt, but sent it skidding on to the floor. It landed at Jake's feet. He bent down and picked it up, bringing the barrel round to face Helga.

She stopped dead.

Jake had never held a gun. It was heavier than he expected. Colder too. With his finger feathering the trigger, he brought up his left hand to support his right wrist.

Helga smiled.

'What are you going to do, boy?' she said. 'Shoot me?'

She took a step forward, round the side of the crate.

'Stay away!' shouted Jake, stumbling back. The gun's barrel was lengthened by what he knew was a silencer. He'd only ever seen one in the movies.

Helga took another step. She was four paces away.

'You don't have the guts,' she sneered.

Jake opened his mouth to speak, to tell her to freeze, but she twisted. Her foot flashed up like a darting snake and the gun jerked from Jake's hand, causing him to pull the trigger. A shower of sparks cascaded over them. Helga turned full circle, crouching low. Her other foot shot out, catching him in the ribs. Jake felt his feet leave the ground, and then pain exploded across his back as he crashed on to the metal steps. It had happened in less than a second.

He opened his eyes. Helga was already at the rear door again. With an elbow, she smashed a panel of Perspex then twisted the handle behind it. Once. Twice.

Jake tried to push himself to his feet, but the pain won and he sank back. He could smell smoke. A panel above him fizzed where the stray bullet had landed.

Helga yanked the door and it opened sideways. Air sucked through the hold as it depressurised, blasting the smoke away. The webbing and any loose straps streamed towards the gap, and seconds later a flurry of papers burst through the hatch from the main cabin and spiralled out like confetti caught in a hurricane. Helga gripped each side of the door, framed by black sky.

'*Do svidanya*,' she said, then winked.

She jumped.

Jake struggled upright, his back in agony, and clambered towards the rear door, gripping the webbing to keep himself steady. The gale slowed then stopped as the plane pressure equalised. Jake reached the open door. A brief, stomach-churning glance revealed the ground wheeling, thousands of feet below. They were getting closer. The roar of the jet stream outside was intense. Jake turned away, gripped the handles of the door and yanked it closed. He spun the handle anticlockwise, sealing the hold.

The din ceased, only to be replaced by a cacophony of alarms and lights from the hazard alert systems.

With no ventilation, smoke was filling the upper reaches of the cargo deck. Jake looked around for a fire extinguisher, but couldn't see one.

He hurried back up the steps into the main cabin. There was smoke there too, but thinner. Powell was still lolling across his seat. Oxygen masks had dropped from the overhead panel and Jake pulled Powell's down further, looping the elastic band around the journalist's head.

Jake left him breathing through his drugged haze,

and made his way back to the cockpit.

'Glad you could make it,' said his dad. 'Take a seat.'

Jake stared at his dad in astonishment. He was casually sitting in the co-pilot's seat and gripping the controls like nothing strange was happening.

'Helga attacked me. She jumped –'

'Just sit down, Jake. I need your help.' He nodded at the pilot's seat, keeping his eyes fixed forward.

The blood-stained pilot was pale as snow. His lips were purple already. Jake struggled against his nausea as he put a hand under the pilot's armpits and tried to lift him. He weighed a ton.

'No need to treat him gently,' his dad said. 'He can't feel anything now.'

He reached past Jake and grabbed the pilot's tie. With one tug, he rolled the dead man off the seat and on to the floor.

Jake ignored the sodden patch of blood and sat in the seat, still warm from the pilot's body.

A red light above the console blinked into life, along with a honking alarm.

'We've got a fire,' said Jake's dad.

'I know,' said Jake. 'That's what I was trying to –'

'You see the transmitter on your right?' his dad interrupted. 'Call in a mayday.'

Jake unhooked the radio. He pushed down the button at the side and spoke into it. 'This is flight er . . . P-O-P twenty-three . . . flying from London Heathrow to St Petersburg. We have a mayday – fire on board.'

Jake released the button. Nothing.

'Do it again, Jake.'

Jake repeated the call. Still nothing.

'Damn it!' his dad said. 'If we can't . . .'

'*Flight P-O-P Two Three,*' said a Russian accent over the radio. '*This is St Petersburg air traffic control. Mayday received. Current status please. Over.*'

Jake's dad leant over and Jake held the transmitter close to him.

'We're twenty miles south of St Petersburg. Fire on board. Pilots dead. Over.'

'*Who is speaking, please? Over.*'

'My name is Steve Bastin,' he said.

'*Repeat please. Over.*'

'I said, the pilots . . .'

The radio cut off, and a spark leapt from the transmitter. A shock jolted through Jake's hand and he dropped it with a cry.

'It looks like we're on our own.' His dad bent forward and tapped a dial.

'Can you land it?' Jake asked.

'If we can find a runway, maybe.'

The acrid stench of smoke reached Jake's nostrils. Grey tendrils were snaking into the cockpit.

They were falling fast. As they burst through a layer of cloud, Jake could make out the patchwork of green fields below. The altimeter read 8,354 feet. Beads of sweat had broken out across Jake's dad's brow.

Suddenly, the plane gave a *whump* and dropped. Jake's stomach rose into his throat. Another alarm joined the fire warning. His dad's knuckles turned white on the steering column.

'Disconnect the starboard engine!' shouted his dad.

Jake frantically searched the control panel. 'Where is it?'

'Above the external pressure gauge,' his dad yelled. 'The two blue panels.'

Jake saw them.

'Pull up the right one, turn the key,' his dad instructed.

Jake opened the panel. There was writing inside. 'DO NOT DISENGAGE ENGINE IN FLIGHT.'

'Are you sure?' Jake asked.

'Just do it!'

Jake turned the key.

The plane continued to drop, but less quickly.

'We need to land now,' his dad said. He eased back the throttle and the plane fell again, this time more steadily.

The fields got closer. The land was flat − farming country. Jake made out forests too.

But no runway.

'Belt up, Jake,' said his dad, coughing. The smoke in the cockpit was thickening.

Jake did as he was told. His hands were shaking so much it took three goes to fasten the straps across his chest. What good would a seat-belt be when they crashed. The smoke brought tears to his eyes.

'You see those two small switches above your head to the left?' his dad said. 'Push the right one down, wait ten seconds, then the next one.' Jake obeyed. As he pushed the first, there was a whirring from somewhere in the fuselage. He flicked the second. There was a crunching and screeching of metal.

'Is that right?'

An LED diagram of the plane in the middle of the controls glowed red at the base.

His dad thumped the control panel with the flat of his hand. 'No!' he yelled. 'The landing gear's wrecked −'

The ground was coming up fast now. The altimeter read 2,059 feet, and it was ticking down in a blur. Jake pulled his T−shirt up over his mouth to help him breathe.

He spotted a distant straight grey line on the ground, sharply to their right.

'There, Dad!' he said. 'A road.'

His dad brought the steering column round and sent the plane towards the only chance they had. Jake didn't know if a plane could land without its gear down. He thought he'd seen it in a movie. But this was real life. They were travelling at nearly 200 miles per hour according to the speedometer. If they hit the ground without wheels, Jake couldn't help thinking they'd come apart like a tin can.

938 feet. Jake stared through the window. He didn't need the altimeter now. He could see the road clearly in the moonlight – and thankfully there were no cars. A row of pylons zipped by at one side and there was a steep bank rising up on the other. The plane was swaying from side to side. There was smoke everywhere. Jake lost sight of the world outside.

His dad eased up the throttle once more and the plane's nose lifted. Jake saw the ground approach, maybe a hundred feet away.

Too fast, he thought. *We're going too fast*.

'Hold on!' his dad shouted.

6

They hit the road.

Jake was thrown up out of his seat with the shockwave that thudded through the cockpit. The nose of the plane angled down into the road, showering sparks up across the windscreen. The noise seemed to fill Jake's head. Metal crushing and grinding, like the scream of a creature torn apart.

The plane tipped to one side as it slid at close to a hundred miles per hour, eating up the tarmac. A crack snaked across the Plexiglas, then it shattered into a thousand pieces, bursting inward. Jake threw up his arms. Everything became white noise – the searing air, the shower of sparks, the random debris bouncing off his body. It all filled his head like floodwater.

The wing must have caught the bank at the side of the road, because the plane jack-knifed round. The whole fuselage rocked sideways and Jake was thrown into the control panel to his side. The sensation of his body being shaken like a rag doll was without pain. Somewhere, deep within his mind, he knew that this was just the adrenalin numbing him – all of this was going to hurt tomorrow.

If it didn't kill him tonight.

He caught a glimpse of his dad's face, twisted with shock and teeth gritted.

Jake's head smacked into something hard. Then he couldn't see anything. His fingers closed on the armrests and he held on grimly.

The plane juddered to a halt.

Jake wasn't sure how many seconds passed. Gradually the creaking and clanging of the decimated plane stopped and Jake was left with the sound of his own breathing and the chorus of dissonant alarms. He was pressed against the wall, his arm on the floor. Or where the floor had been. The cockpit was tilted at a sharp angle. Pain flooded everywhere. Jake checked each of his limbs in turn. Left leg. Flex. Right leg. Flex. Hands. Arms. Neck. All complained, but nothing seemed to be broken.

Jake unclipped the belt slowly and sagged out of the seat. Dizziness swallowed his vision for a second and his knees wobbled. Something tickled his forehead and he knew it was blood. He wiped a red smear away with the back of his hand. His dad was lying on the control panel, his legs still draped across his seat, which had been torn from its housing.

Jake rolled on to his knees.

'Dad?' he said. His dad wasn't moving.

He's dead.

'Dad!'

His dad groaned, his face creasing in pain.

'You're alive,' Jake said.

'Just about.' His dad rolled off the control panel. 'We need to get out of here.'

Following his dad, and leaning against a tilted wall for support, Jake stumbled back into the main cabin. It was unrecognisable. The furniture was scattered to one side, upturned or broken into pieces. The whole place stank of alcohol, burnt plastic and fuel, mixed with smoke that seemed to billow from several places. The back of the plane was gone, and through a tangle of torn metal and wiring Jake looked out into the road behind. He could see the tail-end of the plane, and what looked like half a wing, about 200 metres away. Small fires burnt around the wreckage.

A foot stirred beneath a sofa.

'Powell!' said Jake.

The name brought a moan of recognition from the injured man. Jake and his dad rushed forward and together eased the weight off the journalist's body. His clothes were torn and his left arm was bleeding, but otherwise he looked OK.

'Tell the pilots to go back to flight school,' he said, smiling weakly.

Taking an armpit each, Jake and his dad pulled Powell upright. He winced and hissed when Jake looped his left arm over his shoulder. 'Probably broken,' Jake said, trying to lift from his waist instead.

Together, the three survivors climbed from the back of the plane into the cold night. The tarmac of the road had been chewed up like earth by a plough. The long trail of debris was mostly pieces of the plane, but Jake noticed one of his shin–pads, singed at the edges, discarded on the improvised runway.

Welcome to Russia, he thought.

Less than five minutes later, Jake heard the distant thudding of helicopter blades. In that time, his dad had managed to fashion a sling for Powell from a torn piece of upholstery. Jake found some bottles of water in the dented fridge, which was lying on its side on the road.

'Wait here,' his dad said. 'I'll be back in a moment. There are some things I need.'

He limped along to the remains of the cargo hold and began searching. What was so important? Jake sipped water and shivered. Finally his dad returned, holding the battered box marked 'Personal', just as two choppers with the Popov Industries logo touched down at the top of the roadside bank.

How did they know where we landed? Jake wondered.

One man, wearing a black suit and sunglasses, despite the darkness, ran over. Another four scattered to different parts of the wreckage.

'Is anybody injured?' shouted the first man as he approached.

'Just a broken arm,' Jake's dad said, gesturing to Powell, 'and minor cuts and bruises. The pilots are dead.'

The man nodded but didn't bat an eyelid. 'You will come with us.'

Jake's dad seemed to deliberate for a second, looking first to the shattered plane, then to the helicopters up on the bank. 'Let's go,' he said.

Jake tugged his dad close. 'What are you talking about? We almost died just now. That was Popov's plane! His flight attendant killed the pilots – and she tried to kill you, me and Powell. Now you want to get into one of his helicopters?'

His dad breathed deeply. 'We need to do as this man says, Jake. We can't stay out here in the middle of nowhere.'

'Yes, we can,' said Jake. He pulled his mobile phone out of his pocket. The screen was cracked, but it seemed to work otherwise. And he had a couple of bars of signal. 'We can phone the police. This needs to be reported.'

Popov's man shot out a hand and grabbed the phone.

'Hey!' Jake said. 'Give that back!'

'I have orders from Mr Popov. You *will* come on the helicopter. Now.'

His dad didn't say anything, but instead walked away and climbed the bank to the chopper. Jake saw there was little he could do but follow. Powell, pale and shivering, did the same.

After they were on board, the thug barked something in Russian to the pilot, and the helicopter climbed into the sky.

A sudden boom made Jake's head jerk round. A blast of heat bathed his face as the main part of the plane erupted in a huge fireball.

'What about the bodies?' Jake asked.

'The fuel tanks must have exploded,' said his dad.

'In the front of the plane?' said Powell, raising an eyebrow.

Has my dad destroyed more evidence? Just like the napkin. No traces, thought Jake.

The helicopter circled once and Jake saw the devastation. The wreckage from the plane was scattered over a wide area in smouldering heaps. The 'PI' on the tail was the only part that seemed undamaged. Despite himself, Jake wondered if that was some sort of omen.

As the helicopter glided up and away, Jake couldn't quite

process what had just happened. So many questions. Was Helga working for Popov? She had to be. It was his plane. She followed his orders. But why would the Russian want to kill his new coach and scout? And what about Daniel Powell? The man who turned up at the scene of Andrew Chernoff's murder, almost before the man had died. Was he Helga's real target? It seemed strange that he was now doing a profile on Popov's team after some of the things he'd written about the 'businessman' in the past.

Keep your enemies close, they said.

It was too noisy to think clearly in the back, and despite his mind racing, exhaustion overtook Jake and he only woke when the helicopter rails touched down at a small airfield near some low industrial buildings. From the lead-grey tint of the sky, he guessed it was nearing dawn.

'Where are we?' Jake asked sleepily. His body ached from head to toe.

'The outskirts of St Petersburg,' his dad replied. He was wide awake.

Powell was helped on to a stretcher, then wheeled into a waiting ambulance. Jake was escorted into the back of another. He sat still while a nurse cleaned, then applied mastic tape to the cut on his head. All the time, Popov's henchman watched from behind his sunglasses.

'You may have some mild concussion,' said the nurse. 'Make sure you rest for a couple of days, yes?'

Jake and his dad were ushered into a waiting limousine.

As they drove along an almost deserted motorway, Jake went over the details of the crash again.

'Dad,' said Jake. 'The flight attendant . . .'

His dad shook his head. 'It was a terrible accident. We were very fortunate.'

'Luck had nothing to do with it,' said Jake. He noticed the driver watching him in the rear-view mirror. 'If you hadn't been able to fly the plane −'

'But I was,' his dad said. 'I don't want to talk about it now.'

Jake remembered the carnage in the cockpit, the spattered blood from the co-pilot. *Perhaps I don't want to talk about it either . . .*

Twenty minutes in, the driver spoke for the first time.

'If you look to your right, you'll see the new stadium Mr Popov has built.'

Jake wound down the window to let in some fresh air. The stadium was huge. Bigger than Old Trafford, Jake guessed. With its curved sides and soaring support stanchions, it looked a bit like a giant sixteenth-century galleon at anchor. But this was undoubtedly a modern building. It was all steel and glass, and as the sun rose over the hazy eastern mountains, it glittered like gold. There was still some scaffolding along one wall of the stadium, but otherwise it looked complete.

'It's incredible,' Jake said.

His dad leant past him. 'It certainly is.'

The car took them along a forest road and up a gradual incline. With the cool morning air in his face, Jake wasn't sleepy at all now. They emerged into a clearing with a gate ahead. The driver must have pressed a button, because the gate swung open automatically to admit the car. A building became visible over the brow of a small hill: single storey for the most part, with a single second-floor turret at one end. The whole thing was built of pale wood, with huge floor-to-ceiling windows along the front.

'Welcome to your new home,' said the driver, swinging the limousine round in front. 'Mr Popov hopes you find it adequate.'

Jake slowly exited the car to take in the building better. The forest stretched out below, but beyond that was the stadium, two miles or so downhill, still glittering in the morning rays. Past that were the apartment blocks and offices of St Petersburg, and then the sea.

His dad came to stand beside Jake and put his arm round his shoulders.

'Maybe the worst is behind us. I hope you're glad you came?'

Jake could only nod.

The house inside was a mixture of traditional and modern. The front door opened directly into the kitchen. Jake noticed an espresso maker, juicer, ice machine. Above the oven was an entertainment unit. Jake only noticed it when the screen came to life and Popov's face appeared.

'Hi, Steven,' Popov said, 'and welcome to your new home. I hope you find it to your satisfaction.' While the sight of Popov filled Jake with unease, the crisp image of what he assumed was a videophone call was damn impressive.

Popov continued: 'Karenya is your maid and will help you find your way around the house, and she can also help with any immediate problems. If you need me, any time, day or night, my number is programmed into the in-house systems. For now, rest and explore. I've heard about your accident. I am pleased you are both OK. I've taken the liberty of providing some additional items of clothing and other things to make your stay more comfortable.'

'Thank you, Mr Popov,' his dad said, positioning himself in front of the screen. 'When can I see the stadium and meet my team?'

'I'll send a car tomorrow at ten. For now, *do svidanya*.'

The screen went blank.

Do svidanya. The farewell greeting flashed an image of Helga, perched by the emergency exit, into Jake's mind. He pushed it away.

'Why don't you go and look around?' his dad said, surveying the stack of binders. 'I need to do some work.'

Jake paused in the kitchen doorway. With the new house it was too easy to forget the extraordinary events of the night before.

If it wasn't for their quick thinking and a hefty dose of luck, they'd both be corpses on a lonely road outside St Petersburg. If his dad was a killer, then someone else knew and was also trying to kill him. And without knowing who was pulling the strings, Jake was more in the dark than ever.

He decided to explore the house and grounds. The lounge area, lined with the glass windows, was sunk into the floor. Huge, deep leather sofas surrounded a low slate table. Jake pressed a couple of the buttons discreetly embedded into a side-table. A motor whirred and a large modernist painting along one wall rose into the ceiling to reveal a home cinema system. Plants revolved to reveal four-foot speakers in each corner of the room. Experimenting with the buttons, Jake realised the system contained all the latest movie releases and a catalogue of close to 40,000 songs.

His bedroom was located on the second floor, up a spiral staircase in the turret. In the wardrobe, Jake found several items: jeans, shirts and smarter clothes. All tasteful, high-end fashion. His mother would have approved. The drawers were stocked with brand new T-shirts and underwear.

'How did Popov know my size?' Jake muttered to himself.

There was even a football kit. Jake lifted the shirt up. St Petersburg Tigers, sponsored by Popov Industries.

Lining one side of the room, close to the door of the ensuite bathroom, were several shoe boxes. Converse pumps, Nike trainers, smart shoes in brown and black − and a pair of Predator football boots. The same model worn by Devon Taylor.

This is a bit creepy, thought Jake. *But it's pretty cool too.*

He took a shower and changed out of his filthy clothes.

When he came back downstairs to the kitchen there was a middle-aged woman there with his dad. Plump, with curly brown hair. She was loading food into the fridge, and a fruit bowl was piled high.

'Jake, this is Karenya,' his dad said.

'Hello,' said Jake.

'Hello, Mr Bastin,' she replied with a kind smile. 'Can I make you something to eat?'

Jake didn't much like being waited on hand and foot.

'Please, call me Jake,' he said. 'And I'm fine with an apple, thank you.' He took one from the fruit bowl.

His dad had spread papers across the counter and was reading them closely.

'I'm gonna check out the pool,' Jake said.

His dad grunted absent-mindedly as Jake headed out of the kitchen.

Five minutes later, he was on his fifth lap.

The swimming pool was located beneath the house, almost right along its length. Subdued lighting beneath the water made it feel like a cave lit with candles. As Jake swam, he noticed his body was covered in bruises from the crash.

His dad wanted to work through dinner, so Jake fixed himself a snack and ate it watching *The Bourne Identity* on the home cinema. After the movie ended, he surfed the listings, looking for something else, and came across a documentary about the tragic Busby Babes – eight members of the Manchester United side, managed by the great Matt Busby, who died back in 1958 . . . in a *plane crash*. Jake shuddered as he switched off the TV. He decided to look around the house some more, but his initial wonder had been replaced by persistent unease.

He found his dad sitting at a desk in his bedroom, wearing his glasses. He was stroking his chin, deep in thought. The light from a lamp illuminated the lines of his face. He hadn't noticed Jake watching him. Jake coughed and his dad jumped.

'Hey, Jake, you shouldn't sneak up on your old man like that.'

'I just came to say goodnight,' said Jake.

'Oh, sure. Have a good sleep. Remember we're going to the stadium tomorrow.'

'We?' said Jake. 'You mean I can come too?'

His dad smiled. 'Of course you can. You'll be bored out of your mind here.'

Jake's heart leapt. 'Awesome!' Sure, he wanted to see the stadium and meet the team, but more importantly, he wanted answers. He wouldn't find them in their plush new home. People had started dying the minute they got mixed up with the Russian billionaire and his new football team. Maybe the stadium was the right place for Jake to find those answers.

7

The limousine arrived at ten on the dot and Jake was already outside. The driver was the same guy who'd brought them to the house the day before, but today he introduced himself as Stefan. They cruised down the hill to the stadium, under a clear blue sky. Jake had slept like a log and was feeling great. Even his dad seemed excited as the limousine banked into the stadium's underground car park.

'This place cost four hundred million to put together,' his dad said.

One of Popov's representatives, a thin, suited man called Yvgeny, met them and directed them to an elevator. There were four floors in addition to the underground car park, numbered one to three, and then R. Yvgeny explained that the fourth floor was the exclusive restaurant and helipad, and there was a reception for corporate guests on floor 1. Forty five-star hotel rooms were situated behind the south stand.

The elevator carried them to the second floor and into the area behind the south stand. It was like an office complex, with soft music playing in the corridors, potted-plants lining the walls, and doors leading off to the executive boxes like meeting rooms. There were a few signs that the stadium wasn't quite finished: electricians up ladders and fiddling with wiring in the walls; the general smell of fresh paint.

'I've got back-to-back meetings today,' said Jake's dad, 'so you'll have to keep yourself busy.'

'No problem,' Jake said.

'And don't get into trouble,' warned his dad. 'Remember we're Mr Popov's guests. If you're bored, Stefan can take you back to the house.'

Bored? It would take him most of the day just to explore the second floor.

Jake's dad walked off down the corridor with Yvgeny. Jake was alone. He slipped into one of the boxes. There was a boardroom table and comfy seating. Slatted blinds were lowered over the viewing panel, so Jake flicked the switch to make them retract. As the stadium was revealed, his breath caught in his throat.

It was immense. The stands on both sides were three tiers high. 80,000 capacity, his dad had said. The far stand was dramatically steep, a traditional Kop design, meant to create a thunder of sound when the fans were cheering. There were ten wide passages leading into the stands, four down each side and one at each end. These would filter the fans from the gates and holding areas to their seats. Jake had never seen a ground so empty before. Despite the silence, the place felt heavy with the weight of potential – all the highs and lows it would witness. It was immense.

To the left, above one corner of the stands, was a single glass-fronted structure. It was perched on steel supports, like a giant bird-box. Jake wondered what it could be.

Opposite, above the hotel rooms Yvgeny had mentioned, was the restaurant. Jake could just about make out the tables inside. What a view! A blue and red helicopter suddenly appeared above the stadium and descended on to a landing pad beside the restaurant, the rotors spinning to a stop. It looked like a bird, perched so high up in the stadium.

Someone certainly wants people to see them arrive, thought Jake.

The pitch was a rectangle of lush, flawless green. Two groundsmen were walking rollers along either side, laying down the painted markings. Only one goal was erected, the other lying flat at the opposite end. Jake could only imagine what the ground would be like when it was full; what it'd be like playing in front of that many people. Scoring and hearing the cheers. It gave him goosebumps just thinking about it.

He left the room and padded along the corridor. Most of the spectator boxes were of a similar design, give or take a few metres in size. One was particularly impressive: twice the size of the others, executive leather seating, modern art on the walls. Jake guessed it must be for the VIPs. The door said it was called the Truman Suite.

Jake wandered out into the stands, where the regular spectators would sit, then down the passage that led to the concrete holding areas, toilets and bars that would cater for them before the match and at half-time. His footsteps echoed as he walked.

Further down still, he came to the hub of the ground – the physio rooms and player facilities: a new gym, the running machines and weight apparatus all spotless; the home team dressing room, the door marked with the Tigers' crest. He walked on until he found what he was looking for.

The Tunnel.

Jake's footsteps quickened into a jog as he imagined himself running out on to the pitch on match day. The rectangle of light grew larger as he burst through on to the sidelines. The morning sun was peeking over the tops of the stands. The coaches' dugouts were either side. Deafening silence, interrupted only by the squeak of the roller laying down the throw-in lines. An old Russian with a cigarette in his mouth gave Jake a nod of greeting, then trundled on.

Jake walked out on to the springy turf, turning round and round to take it all in.

What a ground!

His roving eye caught the windows to the offices set into the tiers. A man like Popov could run his whole empire from a place like this, under the guise of simply watching his football team play. Jake felt the now-familiar prickles of curiosity and confusion. Was all of this just a front? He had promised to stay out of trouble, but that didn't mean he couldn't do a *little* investigating, right?

Dad's definitely here for something other than coaching. I want to know what it is.

He took the elevator to the third floor. This was clearly the administrative hub of the stadium. Glass-panelled walls formed offices, and there were computers and desks everywhere. Three people sat hunched over keyboards in one of the offices and Jake heard the gentle tapping of their fingers. The smell of strong coffee reached his nostrils.

No sign of his dad.

Jake headed in the opposite direction, taking a corridor lined with meeting rooms. The floor was carpeted and there were pictures on the walls. He reached a dead end.

He was about to head back when he noticed another set of stairs, with a door at the top. Curiosity got the better of him and he went up. There was a gold panel on the door. *IGOR POPOV, CHAIRMAN*. There was a video camera angled at the door from above, but Jake saw that the connecting wire was hanging free.

I guess Popov's not worried about security.

Jake knocked on the door. No answer. He knocked again.

His dad's words were fresh in his head. *Don't get into any trouble.*

But it was too good an opportunity to pass up. If Popov was his enemy he wanted to know about it. If his dad was hiding something he wanted to know what it was. And if his dad and the Russian were in on something together, then they were crooks, and anything Jake did to uncover their crimes was fair game.

A voice in his head said: *Turn round, Jake. He is your father. Go back downstairs.*

He ignored it, and opened the door.

Inside, Popov's office looked quite old-fashioned: a large leather-topped desk, neat piles of papers, a spot-lamp, a closed laptop computer, an ashtray. There was a door to a small anteroom, where Jake guessed there would be a toilet. A bookshelf, filing cabinets and low cupboards lined the wall nearest to the door. The far wall was a massive window with vertical blinds. When he peeked through the blinds, he realised where he was: the suspended room he'd seen from the stands below.

Jake closed the door behind him. There was a series of black and white pictures along the wall showing the stadium at various stages of completion. The first showed what looked like a disused factory or power station. In the next shot it was being levelled with demolition balls, then foundations were being put in, then you could see the gradual rising of the new stadium. The final picture, in colour, showed Popov standing on the pitch itself. Beside him was a face that Jake would know anywhere: Devon Taylor. He was holding up a St Petersburg shirt with his name on the back. There was another, older man beside him who Jake didn't recognise.

He heard a noise in the hallway. A voice. '. . . my thoughts exactly.'

It was Popov.

Jake's insides squirmed as he surveyed his options.

There were none.

8

In half a second Jake was at the window. He pulled aside the drawn vertical blinds and slid the huge pane across, then using the desk chair, he hopped up on to the sill and climbed out. The ledge was only about four inches wide and extended a few inches either side of the window. Reaching up, he found the top of the window frame with his fingertips. Jake looked down and immediately wished he hadn't. The office overlooked the pitch and the drop to the stands below was around fifty feet, if not more. He pulled the window closed, leaving a tiny crack open so he could hear what was going on inside. Thankfully the blind concealed him.

He heard the office door open, and Popov's voice. 'Of course it will be ready on time, Christian. My people know the price of failure, I assure you.'

Jake edged further out to the end of the sill. Sweat broke out across his forehead. His throat was dry.

'Oh, I know the *price* of failure,' said a deep American voice. 'After all, I'm paying for this, my Russian friend.'

Popov gave a mirthless laugh. 'As you never tire of reminding me. Cigar?'

Jake leant across slightly to peer inside. Popov had his back to the window, and the man opposite was using a cigar cutter to chop off the end of a Cuban cigar almost a foot long. Jake immediately recognised him as the man in the photo with Devon and Popov.

Christian Truman, Jake recalled. CEO of Truman Oil. The stadium sponsor.

'And everything is arranged for the opening match,' said the American, evidently chewing on his cigar.

'Absolutely,' Popov replied. 'The American All-Stars will land mid-week and use the FC Zenit training ground. The Tigers, with Devon of course, are all free of injury. It should be a fantastic game to open the stadium.'

'Yes, yes,' said Truman impatiently. 'I'm sure the spectacle will be fine, but the detailed matters . . . the announcement about Truman Oil . . .'

'Don't worry,' said Popov. 'All of Russia's top business leaders will be here, as will the scientists. *Nothing* can go wrong.'

Jake felt himself frown. Scientists? Just *what* was going on here?

Truman snorted. 'Igor,' he said. 'If there's one thing thirty years in business have taught me, it's that something can *always* go wrong.'

'Tell me, Christian,' said Popov, 'would you like to meet the new coach, Steve Bastin?'

Jake pressed closer to the glass to hear.

'The English footballer?' Truman replied.

'Yes, he arrived yesterday. A great player in his day. A great man.'

Truman nodded. 'By all means, lead the way,' he said.

A moment later, he saw a hand a few feet away through the glass. Popov closed the window completely, and his voice became muffled. 'Remind me to sack the cleaner, Christian.'

Oh no! There was no way back inside the office.

Jake heard the sound of a door closing and waited. Silence. When he was sure they had gone, Jake edged back along the sill, blood pounding across his temples like a jackhammer. As he expected, there was no way he could get back into the office – the window was securely fastened from the inside. He thought about breaking it, but then he was sure to be discovered. He wasn't even sure if he'd be able to break it and keep his balance. The glass was double-glazed.

Jake took a deep breath, forcing himself to calm down and think logically.

The office was isolated, lodged high up from the ground. On either side were sheer windowless walls. Nothing to grab on to. He couldn't go up either. The frame he clung to was less than an inch wide – there was no way he could pull himself up.

That left only one option. Down.

The office would have to be supported on steel legs. Jake let go of the top of the frame, and kept his body pressed against the glass. Thank God there was no wind inside the stadium today.

Gingerly, and keeping his palms on the glass, he crouched down. One wrong move, or a gust of wind to overbalance him, and they'd be scraping him off the stands below. He put one hand then the other on the sill beside his feet, gripped on as tightly as he could. He went down on one knee, then lowered himself off the ledge, so his legs were hanging free into the space below the office.

His shoulders started to burn almost immediately, but Jake hung on. He used to complain about the pull-ups Mr Gill, his old football coach, made him do, but now the tough training was actually keeping him alive.

Jake spied the stanchions that supported the office – thick steel A-frames jutting from the stadium wall. He twisted in the air perilously, trying to swing his legs round one of them. The first time his legs were just short. The second he managed to kick the stanchion, but with each movement his fingers were slipping.

One last time. He swung, stretching his legs, and managed to lock his ankles around the metal support. One hand came loose and for a terrifying moment he thought he'd lost it. But he frantically grabbed the stanchion and held on.

Sweat dripped freely from his head as he got both hands round the metal beam and gripped like a monkey. He half slid, half climbed down the diagonal support. *Nearly there.* When he reached the bottom near the inside of the stadium wall there were plenty of handholds in the form of huge bolts embedded in the cladding. He climbed quickly down then dropped the last six feet. He was right at the back of the top stands. The front of his T-shirt was streaked black from the filthy stanchion.

Jake found an exit passage and made his way back to the lower floors using the stairs. He went cautiously – the last thing he wanted to do was bump into his dad or Popov. The best thing to do would be to head back to the house now, clean up and act like nothing had ever happened.

A door in the passage opened and a group of young men came through, laughing and joking. They were all dressed in the same blue tracksuit, but they were all different nationalities – Jake recognised Lee Po Heng, the Korean international at the front, then behind him Devon Taylor.

Jake stopped dead in his tracks and his mouth hung open.

'Hi,' he said, and immediately felt foolish.

'You know the way to the changing rooms?' said Heng.

'Er . . . yeah,' said Jake. 'Straight along past the gym. It's the third door.'

'Thanks,' said the Korean.

As the players walked past, Devon Taylor stopped and looked at Jake quizzically. He was shorter than Jake had imagined; they were almost the same height.

'Say, kid,' he said in a strong American accent, 'you look a lot like Steve Bastin did twenty years ago.'

This is it, thought Jake. *Make a good impression*.

'He's my dad,' said Jake as nonchalantly as possible.

'No way,' said Devon. He called to the rest of the team, who'd moved on. 'Hey guys, this is the new coach's son.'

The players all stopped and said hi. Jake stuck out his hand. 'I'm Jake.'

The American smiled broadly and pumped his hand. 'Devon. Devon Taylor,' he said. 'Say, Jake, the guys and I are going for a kick-around. Test out this new pitch everyone's going nuts for. D'you wanna join us?'

Training with Devon Taylor! 'You bet!'

*

Devon found Jake a spare kit. As Jake pulled on the jersey with 'Taylor' written across the back, he couldn't quite believe it.

The others were almost as excited as they ran down the tunnel and out on to the virgin pitch. Jake hadn't realised this was the first practice they'd ever had as a team; the Tigers had all been brought together by Popov at short notice. None had played together before. All were under twenty years old.

Not much older than me, Jake realised.

Devon, he knew, was nineteen and a multi-millionaire. His sponsorship deal with Adidas alone was worth nearly five million.

The young Ukrainian, Babiak, carried out a net full of balls for the practice. Each one had the PI logo. They warmed up with some shuttles back and forth across the pitch, then some one-touch, quick-fire passing. Jake hit a pass wide to the Argentine winger, Benalto, formerly of Corinthians.

'Sorry!' he said. 'That was awful.'

'Hey, chill,' said Devon, at his side. 'We all make mistakes.'

'And Bennie makes more than most,' chipped in Calas. He'd played for the Spanish under-21s in the World Cup.

Benalto chased Calas across the length of the pitch, both players laughing.

As the practice went on, Jake started to relax. He kept

his passing short and crisp. *Nothing fancy*, he told himself. *Keep it simple.*

They moved closer to practise short headers in groups of three. Jake was with Devon and the massive French defender called Janné.

'So,' Devon said, 'what's it like to have Steve Bastin as a dad?'

'It's OK,' Jake said. 'I've been mostly living with my mum though. Dad's so busy, y'know.'

'Must be tough,' Devon said. 'I don't see my dad much either.'

Jake concentrated and didn't miss a single header.

After a while Devon called to his team-mates, 'Let's go two on two.' He turned to Jake. 'Jake, you wanna play with me?'

'Sure,' he said, trying to keep his composure.

They squared off against Benalto and Calas, passing back and forth, trying to keep the ball from their opposition. Jake took the ball through Calas's legs and the Spaniard came after him. He clipped Jake's ankle with his boot, but Jake managed to slip a backheel to Devon. Benalto got there first and for a few passes the other two had the ball. When Calas tried to chip a cheeky ball to Benalto, Jake intercepted, taking the ball on his chest and laying it off to Devon. A second later the Argentine came steaming in, catching him full on with a shoulder. Jake sprawled on the turf, his anger flaring. He sprang up, fists clenched.

'What the hell was that!' he shouted.

Benalto raised his hands in a defensive posture. 'Hey, chill out,' he said in a thick Argentinian accent. 'It was just a barge.'

Jake took a step forward and realised the others had turned to face them. Calas was grinning like an idiot.

'Relax, dude,' said Devon, coming up behind him. 'It was an accident, wasn't it, Bennie?'

Benalto nodded.

Jake's own face flushed with shame as his anger dissipated.

One by one, the other players returned to their passing, and he tried to do the same. Benalto went easy on him now, which made it even worse.

When they wound up and jogged over to the upright goal for distance shooting practice, Devon slapped him on the back.

'Looks like you could give your dad a run for his money, Jake.'

It was the greatest compliment Jake had ever received, but he laughed it off. He couldn't help thinking Devon was treating him with kid gloves.

Suddenly, there was a commotion on one side of the ground, and a man was shouting. Two security guards were struggling with a shaven-headed man, prising a camera from his fingers.

'Damn paparazzi,' said Devon. 'How did he even get in?'

The security guard finally got hold of the camera and threw it on to the ground, smashing it into several fragments. The owner brought his hands to his head in dismay, then glumly scooped up the pieces. He was escorted roughly through one of the tunnels.

'Apparently, Mr P wants everything kept private until opening night,' said Devon. 'Paps aren't allowed in till then.'

The goalkeeper, all six-foot-seven of him, was standing between the posts, stretching his massive frame. Australian Brad Emery, formerly reserve keeper for Barcelona. Jake knew he was a great shot-stopper, if not the best tactical player.

'We'll line up thirty yards out,' said Devon. 'One guy lays off the ball, the shooter shoots, then takes on the laying-off role. Got it?'

Everyone nodded.

Jake passed the ball first into Janné's path. The big defender skied it way over the bar.

'This is soccer,' laughed Devon, 'not rugby!'

Janné grumbled and passed a new ball into Devon's path.

He curled a beauty towards the top corner, but it didn't have the pace. Emery tipped it wide of the post with his fingers.

And so they went on, with Jake getting closer and closer to the front of the shooting queue. He didn't know where he was going to put the ball yet. The keeper seemed to fill the goal with his imposing frame, and none of the shooters managed to score.

When his turn came, it was Benalto who knocked the ball to him. Jake decided to go for power rather than finesse. He swung his right boot through the ball, catching it sweetly. It turned slightly in the air and screamed under Emery's outstretched arm. The net ballooned and the other players went wild. They gathered round Jake, whooping and howling, slapping his back and the side of his head.

'Beaten by the coach's son!' shouted Devon at Emery, who was glumly plucking the ball out of the net. 'Great work, Jake.'

Jake nodded and held up a hand to coolly acknowledge the cheers of the Tigers, but inside his heart was close to bursting. *I'll know this is definitely a dream if Keira Knightley emerges from the dugout and pushes past Devon to get to me!*

They finished up the session with some set-piece practice, and after two hours Jake was ready to drop. Though he had the skills, his stamina was no match for older guys who trained five times a week.

His legs were like lead as they headed to the changing rooms. They showered and dressed. Some of the guys were heading into St Petersburg that evening for dinner and Jake almost wished he could join them. They made their way to the car park together.

'You want to come for a spin on the bike?' asked Devon. He pointed to the sleek red Yamaha resting in the parking bay.

Jake gulped. Yesterday he'd only seen Devon Taylor on TV. Now they were . . . well, like mates.

'Dad would want me to stick around, I think,' Jake said.

'No worries,' said Devon. 'I'll have you back here in half an hour tops.' He popped out the spare helmet. 'Come on, it'll be fine. I'm not going to let anything happen to the chief's son, am I?'

So Jake climbed on to the bike and they roared out of the underground car park. It was almost four o'clock and the sun was dipping, but the air was still warm outside. There were several more motorbikes and cars which hadn't been there that morning. They all started their engines as Devon and Jake swept past. *Paparazzi*, Jake thought.

The American twisted the throttle and they left the

entourage behind, but soon they were amongst the rush-hour traffic. Devon pushed the bike between the cars and buses, but the paparazzi bikes kept pace. Two on each, a rider and a cameraman.

They passed grim apartment blocks on either side of the road, then crossed the bridge over the Neva River, which glittered in the late afternoon sun. The city seemed to Jake to be a mass of criss-crossed identical streets. At a traffic light, several paparazzi bikes pulled up beside them.

Devon lifted his visor.

'Why don't you find something better to do?' he shouted.

The only answer he got was more flashes.

As soon as the light was amber, Devon turned the bike left, despite the road sign forbidding such a manoeuvre. The paparazzi were almost all flummoxed, and stalled. Only one bike came after them.

'Lost them!' Devon shouted triumphantly.

The call of a police siren cut through the air.

'We'd better pull over,' yelled Jake. *Dad's going to kill me.*

But instead of slowing down Devon gunned the engine and steered down an alleyway lined with bins. Tall walls towered either side, as he swerved the bike around the trash. The police sirens disappeared.

Looking back, Jake spotted the remaining paparazzi bike

still sitting right on their tail.

This was getting risky. *Running from the press is one thing, but the police is another.*

They turned a couple of times, a left, then a right, and Devon took the bike down several steps. They entered a concrete jungle, daubed with graffiti. The other bike was gone now too, but Devon kept going. The speedometer read forty miles per hour, but it felt faster. Devon turned to look behind, and didn't see the pothole in the concrete.

The front wheel jammed and twisted.

The handlebars jarred sideways and the bike went into a skid. Devon must have squeezed the brakes. Jake's foot went out automatically to stabilise himself, but he fell from the bike, hitting the concrete and rolling. His helmet smacked off the ground.

He heard Devon cry out as he too bailed off the Yamaha. There was a crunch as it hit a lamppost.

'Jake?' said Devon, scrambling over and pulling off his helmet. 'Don't move your neck!'

Jake couldn't help but try. Thankfully, it responded fine. He lifted his head slowly and raised a hand to take off his helmet. The hand was bleeding from a graze and his shirt was torn, but other than that he was unharmed.

A plane crash and *a bike crash . . . what's next?*

'I'm OK, I think,' Jake said. Then panic jolted him. What if Devon was injured? They'd be in a world of trouble. 'Are you hurt?'

'I'm fine,' replied Devon, helping Jake up. 'Which is more than I can say for the bike.'

The front wheel was still spinning slowly. The axle was bent out of shape and fuel was leaking in a puddle from the tank.

'Should we call the police?' said Jake uncertainly.

'Never mind that,' said Devon. 'I got two more of those back at the hotel. Let's just find a taxi.'

Jake stretched his neck as they walked away. 'That was crazy,' he said.

'Damn photographers,' said Devon. 'I can't go anywhere these days.'

That wasn't quite what I meant, Jake thought, but he kept quiet.

They were lost, no doubt about it. Some sort of dilapidated housing estate made up of tower blocks and clusters of low-rises surrounded them. Half the windows were boarded up, and some shreds of washing hung outside on lines, but there wasn't any sign of life. With dark closing in, Jake suddenly felt a shiver of fear.

'I think the main road is this way,' said Devon, pointing to a narrow alley. Jake wasn't at all sure, but he followed anyway. They soon reached a dead end where a mesh fence blocked their path. 'Maybe not,' said Devon.

The scuffle of footsteps made them both turn. Back the way they'd come, two men were blocking the alley entrance.

We're trapped.

Jake couldn't make out their faces, but as they walked towards him and Devon, there was no mistaking the menace in their steps.

9

Jake raised his fists and stepped in front of Devon. The guys were big, but he wasn't going down without a fight. With any luck, he could get in a punch and give them time to escape. He doubted very much that these giants could beat them on foot.

As the men walked out of the shadows, Jake saw that one of them had a nasty pink scar down one cheek, and from the bulges in their jackets he guessed they were both carrying guns.

'Are either of you hurt?' asked one of the men.

Devon put a hand across Jake's chest. 'They're on our side, Jake.' He shook his head at the men. 'We had an accident, that's all. No one to blame.'

'Good,' said the man. 'Mr Popov would be upset if his investment was damaged. Follow us please, Mr Taylor.'

There was no arguing with the tone in his voice. They

followed in the wake of the bodyguards to a waiting black Mercedes. One of the men opened the door.

'What about the bike?' asked Jake as he climbed inside.

'Mr Popov will take care of it,' came the monotone reply. Jake shared a look of concern with Devon, but he just shrugged.

The car threaded through the backstreets of the city and stopped at Devon's hotel on the way back to the stadium. The concierge opened the door for Devon.

'Dad will kill me if he finds out about this,' Jake said. 'Can we keep it quiet?'

'Absolutely,' said Devon. 'My sponsors wouldn't be too happy, either.'

As the car pulled away from the hotel, Jake's mind reeled. How had Popov's men found them? *They were following us.* But even that didn't explain the speed with which they'd been discovered. It could only have been three minutes max between the crash and meeting the men in the alley. Popov's men had been just as fast to the scene of their plane crash.

Clearly Popov liked to keep a *very* close eye on his 'investments'.

They must have used a tracking device. On Devon's bike.

At the stadium, Jake found Stefan asleep at the wheel of

his Mercedes, a copy of the *St Petersburg Times* open on his chest. Jake knocked on the window and Stefan sprang up, wide-eyed.

'Can we go back to the house, please?' he asked.

'Certainly, sir,' said Stefan.

As they drove home, Jake stared absently out of the window. Popov would find out about the crash and how close he and Devon came to getting hurt. But would he tell Jake's dad? Any responsible owner would, and chances are the player would be disciplined. One thing Jake was sure of, Popov was no stranger to secrets. Doing things behind the scenes seemed to be his style.

At home, Jake binned the torn shirt in the outside bins, before showering and treating his grazed hand with antiseptic cream. Hopefully his dad would think it had happened in the plane crash.

As it was, his dad didn't make it back for dinner. Despite Karenya's offer to make him something, Jake made do with some pasta he cooked himself, then he had a proper scout around his dad's room. He was surprised how little guilt he felt at snooping.

He checked the obvious places: beneath the mattress, at the back of drawers and in the top of the wardrobe. He pulled up the rugs and checked all the floorboards, looking for any places his dad might have concealed personal items. Like a gun.

It's got to be here somewhere.

He couldn't find anything. No safe, no suspicious hollow spaces behind the walls.

But the lack of evidence only made him more sure. His dad obviously knew how to keep things hidden.

About eight o'clock, he went down to the pool to loosen up with a few lengths. He was towelling off when he heard the sound of a car in the driveway, then a key in the front door.

Through the pinewood panelling that housed the pool, his dad's voice was clear.

'No, I repeat, Pelé is number one choice. If pushed to substitute I'd recommend Charlton . . .'

Huh? That's some weird game of fantasy football.

'In defence, I'd say go for Butcher, definitely, question mark over Carlos.'

What's he going on about? Terry Butcher last played in the eighties. Roberto Carlos hasn't been good since the late nineties. They were all old footballers.

'. . . any more news on the knee scan? We confirmed malicious intent, yes?'

It sounded like his dad was talking about an injury, but

there was something stilted about the way he was speaking, as though he was reading a script. The conversation became muffled as his dad walked away through the house. Jake wrapped a towel around himself and headed upstairs. He found his dad pacing across the lounge; his eyes flicked to Jake as he entered the room.

'Listen, Seb, I've got to go . . .' He nodded. 'Sure, we'll make sure the dressing room's clean as soon as . . . you too . . . take care. I'll call you at half-time.'

His dad hung up. 'Hey Jake, how was your day? Stay out of trouble?'

'Yes,' Jake forced a laugh. 'I met Devon Taylor and the team.'

'Lucky you,' said his dad. 'More than your old man managed. Back-to-back meetings with the support staff and the sponsor, then a dinner with a load of suits – the great and good of St Petersburg.'

'And you want to bring in Pelé?' said Jake, mimicking holding a phone to his ear.

For a fraction of a second his dad's face hardened, then he broke out into a grin. 'Oh that!' he said. 'Just talking about my all-time fantasy squad with an old team-mate from the playing days.'

'And you'd go for Charlton instead of, say, Van Basten?'

His dad turned so Jake couldn't see his face. 'It's just an opinion, isn't it?'

'Yeah, I guess,' said Jake. 'But Charlton wouldn't get into my top thirty.'

His dad faced him again. The smile was still there, but it was forced. A mask.

'So what was that about the dressing room?' Jake asked.

His dad was already on the way to his bedroom. 'What's with the third degree?' He paused at his bedroom door. 'And the eavesdropping?'

Jake shrugged, trying his best to act casual. 'Just curious.'

His dad stared at him for a long moment before he continued. 'I was just telling Seb that we need to get the facilities sorted out before the first big game. Can't expect players of Devon Taylor's calibre to put up with second-rate changing rooms, can we? See you tomorrow, son.'

'Night then, Dad,' Jake said.

His dad turned to go but then hesitated. 'And, Jake,' he said, his tone clipped and serious. 'I'm dealing with some delicate matters here. It's best if you stayed out of my business.' He shut his bedroom door before Jake could respond.

Jake turned off the lights in the lounge and headed up the stairs to his own bedroom. As he brushed his teeth, the feeling of unease in his stomach grew. His dad didn't know it, but Jake had been in those changing rooms. They were spotless, state-of-the-art. They were quite simply the best facilities he'd ever seen.

And Jake also knew his dad's playing career better than most people. He'd made a point of memorising the result in every league game his dad had played. He could certainly have reeled off all his dad's team-mates.

There wasn't a Seb, or a Sebastian, among them.

Jake set his alarm early for the next morning. He wanted to have another look around before his dad and Karenya got up. He must have overlooked something yesterday. His dad was hiding something and there had to be a clue somewhere among the personal items that he had made such an effort to rescue from the burning plane.

Jake inched open his bedroom door, careful not to make a sound, and tiptoed downstairs. But his dad was already in the lounge, scanning newspapers at the table. He had his reading glasses on and his mobile phone was resting beside him.

If I can get my hands on that, thought Jake, *maybe I can get some answers as to who this Seb is.*

'Morning,' his dad said, glancing at Jake. 'You're up early.'

'Jet lag, I guess,' he replied, shrugging. He grabbed the daily newspaper and flopped down next to his dad, flicking through the paper anxiously. He half-expected to see something about the motorbike chase the day before or a picture of him and Devon making their escape from the paparazzi. But there was nothing.

He heard a door slam outside. Karenya was climbing into Stefan's car.

'Where's she off to?' Jake asked.

'I sent her out to get some fish for dinner,' his dad said. 'I thought we'd eat together tonight.'

'I didn't think you liked fish,' Jake said. 'That's what Mum always said.'

'Jake,' said his dad, suddenly more serious. 'What do you think of Karenya?'

'What do you mean?'

His dad took off his reading glasses. 'I mean, have you seen her behaving oddly? Suspiciously?'

Was his dad worried that Karenya was spying on them?

'It's just,' his dad said, 'I think she's been snooping around a bit. In my room.'

Jake swallowed, fighting the blush that threatened to rise into his cheeks.

'Well, she's a cleaner, isn't she?' Jake said, turning a page of his newspaper and pretending to read.

His dad slipped his glasses back on. 'I guess so,' he

murmured, returning to his papers.

Jake felt his face cool. 'Are you heading to the stadium again today?'

'After lunch, yes. I've got a guy coming to do some work this morning.'

'What kind of work?' Jake asked. 'The place is brand new.'

'Just a few adjustments to make it seem more like home,' his dad said.

'Like what?' Jake folded the newspaper and gave his dad his undivided attention.

'What's with all the questions? A few electronic bits and pieces. Can we leave it at that?' His voice sounded *almost* natural, but Jake detected a slight quaver. His dad sighed and shuffled some papers, then stood up stiffly. 'Want a tea or coffee?'

'No thanks,' Jake said.

His dad started to walk over towards the kitchen, leaving his phone. But at the door he turned, came back to the table, and retrieved it.

'Don't want to miss the boss, do I?' he grinned.

Without the phone, and with his dad in the house, Jake's plans to look for the gun or any other clues had to be put on hold. But that didn't mean he couldn't explore different avenues.

Perhaps his mum could tell him something about this Seb. Or maybe even Chernoff.

Jake tried to call her at eleven, taking his mobile out into the garden. He figured the best time to get her would be in the morning. In the evening it would no doubt be fashion parties until the small hours. Jake wondered if he'd have been better off in Milan.

The phone rang four times, then voicemail kicked in.

'This is Hayley Maguire. Sorry I can't take your call right now. Leave me a . . .'

Jake snapped the phone shut and kicked the head off a dandelion. He hadn't realised his mum had started using her maiden name again, and he didn't really see why it should bother him so much. His parents had been separated for almost ten years, after all.

But that was the point, wasn't it?

I'm still a Bastin. I can't get away from that.

By changing her name, his mother had distanced herself not only from his dad, but from Jake too. The thought brought another flush of anger. His parents had always told him the marriage broke down because of their different career paths, but if his dad had lied to his mum as much as he lied to Jake, he couldn't blame her for walking out on him.

As he pocketed the phone, a sound at the back gate

made him spin round. A bag of some sort landed over the gate and then two hands appeared. A man heaved himself over. Jake took an involuntary step backward.

'Who the hell are you?' he called out.

The man landed heavily and retrieved the holdall. He had a thick beard and shaggy hair. He must have weighed sixteen stone, and was shorter than Jake. If he was a burglar, Jake wasn't scared.

'Sorry, mate,' said the man. He had an accent from somewhere in London's East End. 'This is the Bastin gaff, right?'

'That's right,' said Jake, approaching him. 'And I asked who you are.'

'You must be the youngster,' said the man. 'Lester's the name. 'Ere to check the electrics.'

'Why did you come over the fence?' Jake asked.

'Your dad wanted me to check the cables behind the property. Is he in?'

Cables? I didn't realise there were any.

Before Jake could answer, his dad shouted from the house. 'How are you, Lester? It's been a while, hasn't it?'

Jake's dad was by the back door. He came out with a wide grin and embraced the electrician warmly.

'Certainly has, Mr Bastin,' Lester said.

Jake's dad took Lester's arm and turned him round.

'And you've met my son, Jake.'

'Gave him a scare, I reckon,' laughed Lester. 'Anyway, nothing to report out back. I'll get started around the house if that's OK.'

As the electrician went inside like he owned the place, Jake and his dad followed. Lester peeled off into the lounge and knelt next to his bag.

'We'll leave you to it,' his dad said.

In the kitchen, Jake asked, 'What's he doing in Russia? He sounds like he's from Dalston.'

Jake's dad laughed. He dropped a couple of peeled oranges into the juicer, and switched it on. The kitchen was filled with the sound of a whirring blade. 'Lester's a contractor. Goes where the work is. He did our house years ago when your mum and I were still together. He's a specialist on security systems, too.'

'Won't Popov do that?' Jake asked, having to raise his voice over the noise.

'I wanted a second opinion, you know.'

Jake walked over and switched off the juicer. 'Dad, are we in some sort of danger?'

His dad grinned. 'Don't be daft, Jake. Just keep out of Lester's way, yes?'

Jake headed back to his room. As he passed through the

lounge, Lester was holding something that looked like a paint-roller. He was passing it back and forth across the surfaces of the walls, and he was wearing headphones.

What's he doing? Jake wondered. It didn't look like any piece of equipment he'd seen an electrician use before. But then it was obvious that Lester, behind the banter, was no ordinary electrician. If he didn't know better Jake would have thought the guy was checking for bugs.

Lester was there for most of the afternoon. He repeated the strange search in every room, including Jake's, though he said he was just making sure there were no dangerous circuits. 'You know this Ruski wiring!' he joked. Jake laughed, but he wasn't finding it funny.

Despite his dad's promise, it was dinner on his own again and Karenya made Jake a traditional Russian fish stew. Afterwards, Jake emailed his mum:

Hey mum, how's it going? Hope the shoot is going well. Russia's great, though Dad is very busy. I had a kick-around with Devon Taylor (!) yesterday, but that probably won't mean anything to you. Think the David Bailey of football. Anyway, gotta go.

Jx

Reading over the email, he thought of several new questions he wanted to ask. Small ones like: was Lester really the electrician who'd looked after their London house? Big ones like: did you and Dad break up because of the pressures of football, or because you found out something about him? But all his questions would arouse his mum's suspicions – and if that happened, she'd probably fly straight to Russia and drag him all the way back to Milan. He pressed send.

Lying on his bed, Jake thought of another question, more important than all the others. *Can I trust my dad?*

Perhaps she wouldn't be the best person to answer that.

Jake was awoken by the sound of a raised voice. His dad's. It sounded like he was arguing with someone. Jake checked his watch. 3.14 a.m.

He shivered and climbed off the bed. As he padded down the stairs, the voice was louder still.

'Negative. I'm not ready for that. The window is still open, and until it closes, I keep looking.'

He found his dad standing by the front door, his back to Jake. He was holding the phone to one ear and something in his other hand.

'I've risked everything coming out here. Everything. I'm not leaving without a result. You need to back me up.'

His dad spun round and spotted Jake. A glass of amber liquid sloshed in his hand. Ice cubes rattled inside. On the table, just behind him, Jake could see a bottle of Jameson's.

'Listen, it's late. I've got to go.' He snapped the phone shut. 'Jake,' he snapped. 'I need some damn privacy. Don't sneak up on me like that!'

'You woke me up,' Jake retorted, 'shouting down your phone.'

His dad knocked back the whiskey in a mouthful. 'Don't talk back, Jake, I'm warning you.'

'Or what?' said Jake. 'You'll send me home?'

'That's enough! I knew I shouldn't have brought you here.'

'Just a burden, am I?' Jake shouted. He didn't care if Karenya heard him.

His dad's shoulders lifted, as though he was going to yell back, but then sagged. He sighed.

'I shouldn't have said that, Jake. I'm sorry. It's been a long day. Now I'm trying to sort out a couple of new players from La Liga and Serie A before the transfer window closes, and the owners are talking about cutting spending – bureaucracy, that's all. Can we forget this happened?'

Jake's anger cooled a few degrees. He counted to ten while he watched his dad's face. Getting into a fight wouldn't help him find the truth. 'Sure,' he said.

His dad crossed the lounge and gave Jake a tap on the shoulder.

'I appreciate it, son.' Jake could smell the stale whiskey on his dad's breath. It obviously wasn't the first of the evening. 'Better get some sleep,' he continued. 'Big day tomorrow. Facing the sharks.'

'The sharks?' Jake asked.

'A major press conference,' his dad said. And then, trying to lighten the mood, 'Why don't you come along and make sure your dad doesn't get eaten alive?'

'Yeah, OK.' Jake went back to his bedroom, feeling drained. Before he climbed back under the sheets, he switched on his computer. No reply from his mum, but that wasn't what he wanted to check. He quickly Googled the Russian Premier League transfer regulations.

As the details came up, Jake's heart fell again.

The transfer window had ended a week before. There was no way that phone call had been about new players. Not from La Liga. Not from Serie A. Not from anywhere.

His dad was lying again.

10

The flashes were going off outside the car like muzzle flares. One photographer pressed the lens right up to the window, and Jake wondered if they'd catch anything at all through the tinted glass. Stefan drove swiftly along, seemingly undaunted by the press pack gathered around the vehicle. They were finally admitted to the peace of the stadium's underground car park.

'Thank God for that,' Jake's dad said, fiddling with his tie.

Jake thought his dad looked anxious, though he had no clue why. As a respected elder statesman of the game, and a regular commentator on Sky, he had faced the studio lights hundreds of times. Today, though, his suit looked uncomfortable, his eyes nervous and darting.

They left the car and were led by an escort through to a holding area near one of the larger conference rooms. As a young woman fitted Jake's dad with a microphone and transmitter, the door opened and Igor Popov entered. Jake hadn't seen him properly since their brief meeting in London two weeks before. Popov looked different here, his skin more tanned, his eyes less . . . hungry. 'Jake, how wonderful to see you again! Everything at the house to your satisfaction, I hope?'

'The house is great,' Jake said. *It's everything else that sucks.* He was about to mention the plane crash − the night they'd almost died − but Popov had quickly switched his attention to Jake's dad.

'Ready, Steven? The press are dying to meet the coach.'

'Ready, Mr Popov,' Jake's dad said, standing up and straightening his jacket.

Jake followed them to the conference room. There were no seats left. The front row was all cameramen, kneeling with their equipment. Ranks of journalists lined up behind, all clutching dictaphones and notepads. Jake's dad seated himself with the club spokesman and the assistant coach. A translator sat to one side, relaying messages from English to Russian and vice versa. Jake spotted Christian Truman standing off to one side. Popov joined him.

The questions started off tame enough. One of the journalists asked about team selection. Would the final choices rest with the manager or the owner? Jake's dad replied charmingly that as coach he would always choose the team, but would be happy to discuss it with Popov, who was himself a very good judge of the game. Someone asked about possible rivalry with St Petersburg Zenit, the other big team in the city. Jake's dad replied that the people of St Petersburg deserved a choice, and that ticket prices at the Truman stadium would be competitively priced.

Only when another journalist followed up with a question suggesting that Popov's team should have started the season in the second league, rather than the top tier, did Jake's dad looked flummoxed. The club spokesman leant in to answer, saying that the Russian Football Federation had allowed the move to maintain competition in the country's relatively small Premier League and to acknowledge the obvious investment Igor Popov was dedicating to the great cause of Russian football. The PR person followed up with a request to keep the conversation focussed on football, rather than politics.

The next question didn't need a translator, as the voice that asked it was American.

'Mr Bastin, I have a question.' Jake moved a few paces to the side to confirm the identity of the interrogator was as he suspected – Daniel Powell.

Powell was wearing his arm in a sling, but otherwise seemed to have recovered fully from the plane crash.

He continued: 'Mr Bastin, some commentators have expressed doubt about the relationship between one of Russia's top oil barons, Igor Popov, and an American bastion like Truman Oil. For years, two such business entities wouldn't even have sat across a table from each other. Now they're working together in the "great cause of Russian football". Isn't that *surprising*, to say the least?'

A hush fell over the room, though camera flashes still went off, illuminating the unimpressed faces of the panel. Jake saw Popov speaking behind a raised hand to Christian Truman, who nodded gravely. Popov signalled with his eyes to catch the attention of the monolithic security guards.

'Any answer?' Daniel Powell asked hopefully, before two suited henchmen reached his side. They took hold of both arms lightly, but their body language was anything but gentle. Powell looked half-ready to resist, but instead allowed himself to be led away. He managed to shout one more question before he was taken through a door.

'Did Andrew Chernoff advise you to take this job, Mr Bastin?' Powell called. 'Before he was murdered?'

Jake's eyes glanced at Popov, who gave a curt shake of his head in the direction of the speakers. The PR spokesman stood up beside Jake's dad. 'I'm sorry, Ladies and Gentlemen, this press conference is now concluded.'

The translator relayed the message in Russian and the room broke out in muttering and groans. Jake's dad was ushered out of the side door followed by Popov. Jake watched the crowd talking and gesticulating to one another in confusion. Jake was troubled too. Daniel Powell clearly knew something. There was a web of motives here – something dodgy involving Popov and his dad. Maybe Truman too. So far the web had claimed Chernoff's life, and both pilots. And nearly Jake.

Just which side was Steve Bastin on?

Popov was furious.

'Who does this man think he is?' said the Russian. The vein on his forehead was prominent and a lock of his dark hair had fallen out of place. They had retired to an anteroom. Christian Truman, Igor Popov, Steve Bastin and Jake. Jake was pretty sure he wasn't actually allowed or wanted in the anteroom, but he had followed too closely for them to shake him off.

'I invite him here, to my country, and my stadium,' Popov was saying, 'and *this* is how he repays me. By embarrassing me in front of the press!' He held out his hands towards Jake's dad, who was looking at his mobile phone. 'Steven, what should I do with this man? In the Soviet days, well, that was different. I would have . . .'

Popov stopped talking abruptly and fixed Jake with a stare.

'I get carried away. Nothing can be done now. The game is on Saturday and then everything will be OK again. I'm very sorry, Christian, that this countryman of yours has been allowed to spoil the day.'

Christian Truman nodded. 'That's quite all right, Igor,' he said in his Texan drawl. 'We have plenty of problem journalists Stateside, too.'

Both men continued talking, but Jake's dad seemed distracted. Jake watched as he turned away from Popov and Truman and checked his phone for messages. He tapped a few buttons and then shoved his phone in his jacket pocket.

'Everything OK, Steve?' Truman asked, finally noticing that Jake's dad had disengaged from their conversation.

'Gentlemen, I've just remembered I left some documents in the car. Will you give me a moment?'

You're up to something right now, thought Jake as he watched his dad slip out of the room. Jake waited a few seconds and then excused himself as well.

The lift doors were just closing on his dad. Jake sprinted to the stairwell. He took the steps three at a time, vaulting over the rail where it turned. He covered the three flights down to the car park in less than ten seconds, and shoved open the door into the underground area. Half a second later, the elevator pinged, and the doors opened.

Jake ducked behind a column and tried to still his breathing.

He leant out and saw his dad stride purposefully across the parking bays. Jake's blood was pulsing across his temples. His dad was almost at the car when another figure stepped out in front of him. Powell. What was he doing down here? Hadn't security escorted him out? The American's lips were moving, but Jake was too far away to hear what he was saying.

Suddenly Jake's dad lunged forward, shoving Powell in the chest. The journalist crashed backward on to the bonnet of the car, with Jake's dad's hands at his throat. Jake couldn't help the gasp of astonishment that left his lips.

His dad was leaning over Powell, who squirmed helplessly underneath him, one arm still in the sling. Jake didn't know what to do. Should he run over and help? Let his dad know he was spying on him? His dad raised a fist.

Jake stepped out, but the punch never came. Instead Daniel Powell stopped writhing. Jake had seen his dad provoked before, on the pitch. Never, in all that time, had Steve Bastin ever raised his hands to hit someone. They used to call him a gentle giant. Despite all the abuse that came his way, all the niggling kicks and dirty tactics from opposing players, nothing could rile him to react. Yet here he was, behaving like a thug on the street.

Jake crouched low and darted behind a row of cars. Thankfully the parking bay was poorly lit, so he could stick to the shadows.

He peeked through the windows of a 4x4 and saw that Powell was now standing shakily in front of his dad, straightening his shirt with his good hand. Jake's dad's fists were still clenched on Powell's collar. Their faces were three inches apart, and Jake had to strain to hear the low voices.

'. . . a lot we have to talk about,' Powell was saying.

'Just stay away from me,' Jake's dad replied. '*And* my son.'

'We both have a job to do,' said Powell. 'I intend to do mine.'

Jake's dad slammed Powell back on to the bonnet. 'Don't push me, Powell,' he shouted. 'This is bigger than you, and you'll get hurt.'

Jake couldn't hear what the American said back, but his eyes caught a swift movement. Powell reached into his pocket. *A gun*, Jake thought. But it wasn't. The object looked like a stick of chewing gum.

In a single, fluid motion, Powell dropped whatever it was into the side pocket of Jake's dad's jacket.

'OK, OK,' said Powell. 'You're right. I'll keep my distance.' Jake's dad seemed to relax.

They separated. Powell held up his palm in a defensive

posture. 'I'm sorry, Mr Bastin. I guess my instincts got the better of me.'

'Be careful, Powell,' Jake's dad said. The words were almost more threatening for the flat tone in which they were uttered.

Powell just nodded and walked off towards the car park exit. Jake's dad stood motionless until Powell had left. Then he slammed his fist on to the bonnet of the car. 'Damn it!' he shouted. The sound echoed off the concrete walls.

Jake used the opportunity to make his exit. He dashed towards the stairwell, slipped through the door and hurried up the stairs. There was too much to take in.

First my dad's lying to me, now he's threatening reporters. Can this really be him?

Jake stepped back out into the conference room, where the last of the journalists and cameramen were clearing out, heading down to the pitch to set up for the practice session. His dad arrived in the lift a few seconds later. He was carrying a document case and looked surprised to see Jake.

'What are you doing in here?' he asked.

'Couldn't hang out with Popov and Truman all day. I got the feeling they wanted to be alone,' Jake replied. 'What took you so long?'

His dad grinned. 'Y'know, couldn't remember for the life

of me where the car was parked.' He tapped his temple with an index finger. 'Guess the brain is getting old like the rest of me.'

He walked over and mimed a light punch to Jake's chin. 'Sorry if I seem anxious, Sport. It's just the job. It'll be all sorted soon.'

Jake decided to return his dad's new-found affection and lay it on thick too. He hugged his dad, squeezing hard. It was an awkward embrace. His dad stood motionless for a second but then leant in and patted Jake on the back. But Jake had an ulterior motive. He slipped his hand into his dad's pocket and felt for the object.

They drew apart.

'Anyway, Jake, I've got to get changed for practice. Why don't you go to the stadium cafeteria, get something to eat. I don't think the main restaurant is open yet.'

'Sure thing, Dad,' said Jake.

'And, one more thing –' his dad started.

But Jake finished the thought – 'Stay out of trouble?'

His dad grinned. 'You know me too well.'

Do I? Jake thought as he watched his dad walk away. When he was on his own, he opened his hand to look at the object in his palm. A computer pen-drive. What was on it? And why had Powell slipped it to his dad?

11

Jake had no intention of going to the cafeteria.

The last of the players were heading out towards the pitch. A security guard stood outside his dad's office.

'Steve Bastin – my dad – said I should wait for him here,' he said, trying to sound as natural as possible. The guard nodded and waved him through.

Jake switched on the laptop on his dad's desk and waited for it to boot up. None of this made sense. One moment Daniel Powell was about to get his jaw broken, the next he was handing over information to Jake's dad. Jake was pretty sure his dad hadn't noticed the pen-drive being slipped into his pocket – Powell had done it so covertly – so what was going on?

He wasn't surprised to see that the screensaver was an image from his dad's playing days. It was the team photo of the 1988 England squad. Steve Bastin, square-jawed and long-haired, stood in the back row alongside his team-mates. It must have been taken a few days before he was stretchered off with the torn ligaments that ended his career. Jake shook away any sympathy. His dad was no legend.

Jake inserted the drive into the USB socket. The drive contained a single pdf file, called 'Elisandos'. Jake double-clicked on the document icon.

The file was an article from *O Globo*, a Brazilian newspaper published in Rio. There was a picture of a round-headed man with a neat beard. Beside it was a shot of a forty-foot yacht being towed by a coastguard vessel. The man's picture was labelled 'Prof. Hector Elisandos'. Jake knew a little Spanish, but no Portuguese. He couldn't understand the article, but he recognised one name immediately. Christian Truman.

Jake opened a translation programme from the Internet, highlighted the article text and dropped it into the programme. It took the computer a couple of seconds to convert the article into English. It wasn't perfect, but it gave him the gist:

Hector Elisandos was the world's leading authority on tidal energy. His yacht had been recovered off the coast of Jamaica with no one on board. Recently he'd been consulting for Christian Truman on energy projects.

There was a knock at the door. Jake quickly flipped the laptop closed. 'Come in,' he said.

It was Benalto, the Argentine player. His forehead was coated with a sheen of sweat and he was breathing heavily from training.

'Oh, hello, Jake,' he said. 'Have you seen your father?'

'I thought he was with you,' Jake said.

'No,' said Benalto. 'We look for Devon also. I thought they are here, but I see no. Sorry to interrupt.'

He closed the door and was gone.

Jake opened the computer again and continued to read. Apparently, no body had been recovered, but the suspicion was that Elisandos had drowned. There was a quote from Truman that said that he was devastated by the loss of such an eminent scientist, especially because his research seemed to have been lost with him.

Jake closed the file, then opened the Internet and searched for Elisandos. It was strange: none of the major English-language newspapers seemed to have picked up the story of the disappearance. Perhaps Elisandos wasn't such a big deal, after all. So why had Powell slipped the story to his dad?

Jake deleted the history files of his search. He didn't want to leave any sort of trail that his dad might pick up on. He took in the screensaver a final time. His dad's smile seemed so innocent . . . Shaking any thoughts of loyalty away, Jake shut the computer down and pocketed the pen-drive as he left the office, walking straight into Devon Taylor.

'What the –' he began. 'Oh, Jake, it's you. Sorry, dude.'

'Hey, Devon,' Jake replied. 'Bennie was looking for you.'

'I was seeing the physio,' said Devon.

'Everything OK?' Jake asked.

Devon slapped his right thigh. 'Hope so. Slight tear to my hamstring last year. It's recovered, but still aches after sprints.'

'The first game's only a couple of days away. Will you be fit in time?'

'Should be. If your dad doesn't bench me for being late for practice.'

Jake laughed, but inside he felt only sadness. If Devon only knew that his dad didn't care about football as much as he pretended. 'Better get out there then.'

Jake followed Devon out to the pitch. It took him a few seconds to realise what was different: the sky wasn't there. The stadium's retractable roof had been drawn across like a gigantic shroud. Instead of the sun, hundreds of dazzling spotlights illuminated the pitch. Jake stood open-mouthed.

'Wow!' he said. 'What a place to play.'

'Sure is. And it looks like I'll get away with being late,' Devon smiled. Jake looked over to where he was nodding. The players were all gathered round the assistant coach near the far goal, but his dad was nowhere to be seen. Devon jogged off to join them.

Jake was left alone on the sidelines. Where *was* his dad?

Across the other side of the pitch, above the tiers, was the Truman Oil sponsor box. Jake could tell that its view of the pitch was almost as good as the one from Popov's office. Two figures were standing together behind the glass, and Jake squinted up. Truman and Popov. The Russian was gesturing over the pitch with one arm in a wide sweeping gesture. In his other hand he held a mobile phone to his ear.

A tannoy crackled into life, and someone spoke in Russian. A few of the security guards looked up, and so did the assistant coach. Then the message was repeated in English: 'For health and safety reasons, please leave the football pitch. We will shortly be testing the stadium roof. I repeat, please vacate the football pitch.'

Some of the players drifted towards the opposite touchline. Devon and Janné came towards Jake.

'Why do we all have to stay clear?' asked Janné.

'In case something goes wrong, I guess,' said Jake.

'Nothing will go wrong,' Devon said. 'They spent millions on the technology.'

The field is clear, boomed the tannoy. *Proceed with testing.*

The spotlights flicked off. Suddenly it felt like they were in a giant cave. It was dark as night.

'Bloody hell, I almost missed it!' said a voice. Jake spun round to see his dad limping quickly to the edge of the pitch. 'Beats Wembley, huh?'

Jake was about to answer when the clanging of machinery interrupted him. A pale crack appeared where the roof panels parted, sending shafts of light on to the centre circle. As the mechanism whirred, the two wings retracted slowly.

A piece of debris detached from the edge of one of the wings and fell off. Straightaway, Jake knew something was wrong. A fraction of a second later, he realised it wasn't debris at all.

It was a body.

Legs and arms spiralled as it plummeted, turning over and over. Jake turned away, but heard the sickening thud as it smacked into the turf. Bile rose into his throat. What followed was a blur. He didn't want to see, but his legs carried him towards the centre circle anyway.

He heard someone shouting, 'No, Jake!' His father.

But Jake was close enough to see the limbs bent out of shape. The neck at an impossible angle. Blood colouring the clean white halfway line. No first aid could help this person. Then he saw the face, pale and lifeless.

Jake fell to his knees and his nausea overcame him. Retching from the depths of his guts, he vomited on to the grass.

The dead man was Daniel Powell.

12

Strong arms seized Jake's shoulders and pulled him from the scene. His dad.

Jake wanted to push him away, but he didn't have the strength.

An accident?

Suicide?

Security guards streamed past on either side. 'It's nothing,' they were saying in Russian. 'Nothing to see.'

Jake saw Janné's face, contorted with horror. Devon Taylor's eyes were wide with shock.

Murder.

Jake knew he was right. Daniel Powell had been murdered. He remembered his dad's last words to the journalist, uttered so coldly: *Be careful, Powell.*

Jake's skin prickled with fear and the sickness took him again, coiling in his guts like a snake. He puked in the tunnel, spattering the concrete floor.

'Get it all out, son,' his dad said.

A man and a woman, both in police uniforms, rushed towards the pitch. A siren blared in the distance. Jake wanted to grab one of the officers, tell them what he knew, but his dad kept ushering him forcefully into the belly of the stadium. They reached the lift and stepped inside. Jake wiped his mouth and stared at his reflection in the mirror on the wall. He looked terrible: pale, sweating. Behind him his dad was stepping impatiently from foot to foot. He was stabbing at the elevator button. 'Oh, *come on!*'

Why is he in such a rush?

The doors swished closed.

His dad said something Jake didn't hear. His world was spinning.

'I *said*, are you OK, Jake? Talk to me.'

'I . . . I'm OK,' Jake said.

He couldn't tear his eyes from his dad's hands. He kept asking himself: *Did those hands take Daniel Powell's life?*

They were in the car and driving away from the stadium just as another ambulance arrived, sirens on.

There's no need to hurry, Jake thought, remembering Powell's broken body. Then he felt guilty. Weren't they fleeing a crime scene? His dad was on the phone, talking to Popov.

'I thought it was best to leave,' he was saying. 'There's no way we could carry on practice after that. Tell our driver to go home.' A pause. 'Yes, tomorrow. Bye.'

'Dad,' Jake said. 'Shouldn't we go back? I mean, the police . . . they might want to talk to us.'

He guessed the answer before his dad even spoke. 'The Russian police can't be trusted, Jake.'

A brush-off. He wasn't going to let his dad get away with it.

'Yeah, but after the plane crash, and him getting thrown out of the press conference . . .'

'I said forget it,' his dad said curtly. He was driving calmly, but quickly, nosing the Mercedes from lane to lane. Jake checked the speedometer: almost eighty miles per hour. His dad spoke again: 'This isn't like the UK. A lot of the police force here are in the pockets of Russian gangsters.'

'Like Igor Popov?' Jake sneered.

As soon as the words left his mouth, he regretted it. His dad swung the car across the inside lane of traffic and slammed on the brakes. Jake's seatbelt tightened across his chest and he was thrown back into his seat.

His dad craned his head round, almost as though he

expected to see somebody seated in the back of the car. Then he fixed his eyes on Jake.

'What the hell do you mean by that?' His skin was bloodless with fury, or fear – Jake couldn't tell which.

'All I'm saying,' said Jake, meeting his dad's eyes, 'is that I know a lot more than you give me credit for.'

'Well, stop saying.' His dad looked around again and then whispered. 'You never know when someone may be listening.'

They were silent. The only sound was the hum of the air conditioning. Jake thought back to Lester the electrician's work at the house. Now it made sense. His dad *had* asked him to search for listening devices. And he wasn't discussing a fantasy football team when Jake overheard him on the phone. He was talking in some sort of code, using old footballers' names. But why?

His dad pulled out into the traffic. They were almost at the house when he gave a heavy sigh.

'Mr Popov's been good to us, Jake. This job is important. It's not just about football, it's about cooperation. East and West. A new beginning.'

'What do you mean? How can you work for such a crook?' Jake asked.

His dad's head whipped round. 'You mustn't talk that

way about Mr Popov . . .' He seemed to collect himself as he looked back at the road. His voice was quieter. 'Mr Popov is a successful businessman. And in Russia they do things . . . differently.'

'Like kill people? You know that Powell was murdered. And Chernoff, too.'

'No, I don't!' his dad said with sudden vehemence. 'Jake, back off, Andrew was my friend.'

Jake was taken aback by the ferocity of his dad's words, but he felt a tingle of excitement too. At least he was getting somewhere.

'And Powell? Was he your friend?'

His dad took a deep breath and when he spoke again his calm was restored. 'He might have jumped.'

Jake recalled the figure cartwheeling from the sky. 'I think he was dead already,' Jake said. 'We should have stuck around to find out.'

His dad stopped the car in the driveway and turned off the engine.

'We can do without the bad publicity,' he said. 'People are already waiting for Popov to fail. The last thing he needs is for the police to get in the way. Not with the big game at the weekend.'

Jake wasn't sure that was the answer he was looking for.

In his dad's face he saw only anxiety, but how could he be worried about the game after what had just happened?

'Dad,' said Jake. 'Stop lying to me. I'm not a kid any more.'

His dad swung open the door and climbed out.

'I know you're not, Jake. But there are still a lot of things you don't understand.'

'How *can* I if you're so secretive?' Jake said.

'Just drop it, son,' said his dad. 'If you don't keep your nose out of my business, it could be dangerous.'

He walked towards the door of the house.

'What's that supposed to mean?' Jake shouted after him.

His dad walked inside without answering.

Was he threatening me? Jake asked himself. He leant against the car and rubbed a hand through his hair. The image of Powell falling and the dreadful sound as he hit the pitch replayed over and over in his head.

Is that the price for crossing the great Steve Bastin?

The next morning Jake woke feeling exhausted after a fitful night's sleep, but his dad seemed bright-eyed and raring to go at breakfast. It was like he'd forgotten the awful events at the stadium.

'Today should be great, Jake. Christian Truman has

invited us over for lunch at his ranch. A real treat.'

Jake swallowed a mouthful of toast. 'Truman has a ranch in Russia?'

'Apparently so – his oil company has land all over the world.'

'Wherever there's oil to pillage, I guess,' said Jake.

His dad laughed and for a moment it was like the last two weeks hadn't happened. 'Actually, Truman Oil are looking into all sorts of different resources, not just fossil fuels,' his dad said.

Jake remembered the article about Hector Elisandos. The pen-drive was hidden in his football boot.

'Like tidal energy?' he said, as nonchalantly as possible.

His dad shrugged. 'I don't know about that. But wind power, for sure. His whole ranch runs off a wind generator, apparently. Some kind of advanced technology. It's near a place called Pogoli, inland along the river.'

Jake didn't particularly want to spend the day traipsing around Truman's ranch. Anyway, with his dad out of the way, there'd be a chance he could speak to his mum. Get some answers.

'I think I might give it a miss,' he said. 'I feel pretty tired after yesterday.'

His dad looked obviously disappointed but said,

'Sure, you take it easy then.'

Jake climbed off his stool and was about to head back to his bedroom when a car horn went off outside. His dad checked his watch.

'They're early,' he said.

'*They?*' Jake repeated.

'That's right,' said his dad. 'Mr Truman's invited the whole team. It's a bonding exercise. I doubt they'll all come though. Are you sure you don't want to join us?'

Jake rushed to the window. There was a coach parked further down the driveway, with tinted windows. Devon Taylor was standing by the side of it, speaking on a mobile phone.

There's no way I'm missing this, Jake thought.

'I'll get my things,' he said.

The coach headed east away from St Petersburg, staying on the southern side of the river until they reached a massive, four-lane bridge. Jake's dad was right – they really didn't need a coach this size as only half a dozen players had come along. Jake supposed millionaire footballers needed lots of room.

The mood on the coach was sombre. Powell's very public death seemed to have taken some of the spark out of the players. It wasn't surprising that Popov wanted to get them away from the press for a day.

They took a service road off from the highway and headed down a track through dense forest until they reached a tall mesh gate. There was a wooden cabin to one side, from which armed security guards emerged. After a quick chat with the driver, the coach was waved through.

'It's like a military facility,' said Jake to Devon.

'Truman has something pretty special going on out here,' replied Devon blankly. 'State of the art.'

The forest ended abruptly and the players were out of their seats looking through the windows on one side of the coach. Jake joined them.

Truman's ranch house was a sprawling, two-storey building, painted white, with arched gables and wooden facings. It looked like it had been shipped timber for timber, from somewhere in the southern United States. Jake could not imagine anything that would look more out of place against the bleak Russian landscape that was its backdrop. The same blue and red helicopter that had landed at the stadium was resting on a raised plateau in front of the house.

Christian Truman himself stood on the sheltered veranda, wearing a Stetson and cowboy boots. Beside him stood a smaller man with curly hair and glasses, dressed in a blue casual shirt and straight jeans. A row of stables backed one side of the building. Beyond the trees on the far side of the house, Jake made out two huge wind turbines, each with four wide blades.

They climbed off the bus into the warm sunshine.

'Howdy, fellas,' said Christian Truman. He greeted each of them in turn, pumping Devon Taylor's hand the longest. *A fellow American*, Jake thought.

'Gentlemen,' Truman continued, 'there'll be time for some lunch later, and some horse-trekking too if the coach allows it.' He smiled a wide, white smile at Jake's dad. 'But first, there's going to be a big announcement prior to the game tomorrow. We've kept it under wraps until now, but I want you to be the first to know.' He puffed out his chest and hooked his thumbs in his belt. 'My family has been drilling in America since the 1920s, and abroad since 1964. But the world has changed, and Truman Oil is changing with it. Fossil fuels are only one part of the global energy solution. Today, I'm going to show you just part of our new direction. It's time for you to see where the money for football comes from.' He gestured to the man beside him. 'This is Dr Ian Dowden, and I'm pleased to have him on board. Some of you may have heard of him. His papers at MIT have revolutionised technology for sourcing wind power. Because of Ian, wind power is more efficient and cleaner than ever before.' He pointed towards the huge stationary blades over the treetops. 'What you see here is just a prototype, but those turbines provide over 10,000 times more energy than I need to run my ranch. A hundred would provide enough energy to run . . .' He waved his hands. 'Well, I'll let Dr Dowden tell y'all himself. Fellas, I'll see you later.'

Truman headed back towards the house and Dr Dowden stepped forward. He looked a little nervous, and his hands smoothed down either side of his trousers, as though he was checking for something in his pockets.

'Gentlemen,' he nodded briskly, 'if you'd like to follow me.'

With that, he was striding off along a track towards the wind turbines. Jake fell into step with the rest of the players, but when he looked round he realised his dad wasn't with them. Glancing further back, he saw that his dad was talking earnestly with Truman. Popov was there too, seemingly happy and relaxed in casual clothes. He must have been waiting in the house.

The doctor led them in single file along a narrow footpath and soon the masts were looming above them. Up close they looked even bigger, like giant conifers soaring into the sky. Only these were painted pristine white. Jake knocked on the side and heard a hollow thud.

'A type of fibreglass,' said Dr Dowden. 'Modified at molecular level for increased durability and stability. Once these turbines are in operation, the maintenance will be minimal. It means we can place them in remote places without worrying about calling in the electrician.' He smiled. Jake guessed that was as close to a joke as MIT scientists came.

They reached a double door.

'As Mr Truman was saying,' Dowden continued, 'a hundred of these sails will be able to power a city the size of Paris.'

Janné interrupted. 'I didn't think wind power could be so strong.'

'It wasn't,' said Dr Dowden, pushing up his glasses, 'until now. Welcome to the control room, Gentlemen.'

He pushed open the door and they found themselves in what looked like a laboratory. There were banks of buttons, levers and flashing lights on three sides of the room. Two orderlies in white coats were studiously attending to monitors and gauges. In the centre of the room was a semi-transparent panel with a diagram of the two towers and various LEDs blinking. Everything was spotless.

Jake found it hard to take in. This seemed like a miniature version of Mission Control at NASA. By the looks of the players, they were astounded, too. On the far side of the room was a glass panel leading into what seemed to be an empty white chamber.

'What's in there?' Jake asked.

'That's the test chamber,' said Dr Dowden. 'We can channel the power from the blades above. With a flick of a switch, the air inside this chamber can shift from a gentle summer breeze to hurricane gales.'

'Can we see how it works?' Devon asked.

'I thought you'd never ask,' Dr Dowden said. He called to one of the other scientists. 'Hans, shall we run a test for the visitors?'

The male orderly nodded and quickly began flipping switches. Dr Dowden unlocked the test chamber door with a code. It hissed open.

On the diagnostic panel in the centre of the room, both sails blipped into life, showing that the real blades above the trees were turning.

Jake and the others gathered at the glass window. At one end were two fans, each ten feet across. At the other was a wall that seemed to be made of sharp rods, all about three feet long, sticking out like an upturned bed of nails.

'What are those?' Jake asked and pointed to the menacing spikes.

'Those are high-tensile rods,' Dr Dowden replied, seeming pleased at the interest from his audience. 'The whole chamber is magnetised, generating a current from the energy created by the turbines.'

'In English?' joked Devon.

'It's also good for drying your hair,' said Dr Dowden. That one didn't get a laugh either.

Dr Dowden closed the door behind him. His voice came over the speaker. 'Just show them Level One, Hans.'

The scientist flicked two switches and turned a dial. 'Level One initiated,' he said.

A display above the chamber read *Level 1*. The blades at the far end of the chamber began to turn. A fraction of a second later, Dr Dowden's hair stirred. 'Level One can generate enough energy to power the floodlights at the new stadium,' said his tinny voice. 'The generator can run consistently at Level One for up to six months. Dependent on the wind, of course. Show them Level Two, please.'

Hans twisted the dial. Now Dr Dowden's shirt was flapping. 'By changing the angle of the turbine blades we can adapt for different weather conditions.' He made a twisting motion with his arm to demonstrate. 'And deactivate please, Hans.'

The wind seemed to pick up. The digital display said *Level 3*.

'Repeat, deactivate the turbine,' said Dr Dowden.

The figure switched to *4*.

Jake and the others all looked to Hans, but he was frantically flicking switches.

'Dr Dowden,' he said, 'there seems to be some sort of malfunction.'

Level 5.

Dr Dowden's tie whipped behind him, trailing like a banner.

'Override,' he said. Panic was creeping into his voice.

'Override unsuccessful,' Hans said, equally panicked.

Level 7.

'I'll get help,' said Devon, breaking away from the group.

'Get him out!' Benalto said. He reached the door and tried to open it, but it seemed stuck.

'The code!' Jake shouted, remembering the keypad. 'Dr Dowden, what's the code?'

The doctor reached the other side of the door. 'Zero, seven, one, one,' he shouted back.

Jake punched it in, but a red bar flashed.

Level 8.

Dr Dowden's glasses were torn from his face and smashed into fragments among the conducting rods. Jake noticed his lips had turned blue. The temperature inside must be dropping.

Hans had come to the door now and punched the code again. No effect.

'What can we do?' said Jake.

Level 9.

Dr Dowden's feet suddenly went from under him and he scrambled on the floor, fighting against an invisible current of air. He managed to grip part of the door frame.

Hans looked terrified, so Jake grabbed his shoulders. 'Hans, there must be some way of shutting this down!'

The others were urging Dr Dowden to hold on. The scientist couldn't speak, but Jake could read his eyes. They were pleading for help.

'The sails are controlled by the wind.' Hans stared wide-eyed at Jake. 'They only switch off when there's no breeze.'

'There must be another way,' Jake said. 'Think!'

'Outside. On the mast itself. An override lever behind a panel. Near the top,' panted Hans. 'But it's impossible to do when the sails are spinning.' Hans looked at Dr Dowden, still clinging to the door frame. 'There's no time.'

Level 10.

Without looking back, Jake ran for the door.

13

The air outside was warm, but Jake's blood felt cold. He immediately spied the simple ladder running up the side of the mast. At the top, the blades were spinning serenely – nothing to hint at the terror inside the control room.

Jake sprinted to the bottom of the ladder and began to climb, hand over hand, as quickly as he could. Every second the turbine would be blasting harder into the test chamber, and the temperature would drop further. If Dr Dowden let go, his body would be punctured by the conducting rods. Jake felt sickened by the thought of such a gruesome end.

By the time he was level with the treetops, his arms were starting to burn. A quick glance up confirmed he was more than halfway there. The wind from the immense blades buffeted over him.

To one side, he could see the roof of Truman's house. Devon should be there by now. He would have warned everyone what was happening just a couple of hundred metres away. Jake pushed on.

He was close to the bottom of the blades now.

He looked down. A mistake.

The forest floor seemed tiny and he could see the players, anxiously staring up. They were shouting words he couldn't hear. Jake had never been afraid of heights, but the sheer terror in the faces below seemed to infect him. Suddenly his legs were like jelly, and the sweat across his forehead turned icy. He forced himself to reach up again.

And there it was: the panel. Daubed in Russian and English: MANUAL OVERRIDE: OPERATE ONLY IN CASE OF EMERGENCY.

Jake pulled open the hatch. Inside was a T-shaped handle. He grabbed it. It didn't move. He tugged harder, but still the lever wouldn't budge.

'Come on!' Jake shouted. He couldn't fail now.

Bracing himself, he yanked as hard as he could. The lever flicked over. He felt a flood of relief as he heard a sound like a ratchet tightening and the blades slowed immediately. Then Jake felt his weight tipping – the handle had come off in his hand! He reached for the rung, but it was too late.

Jake pushed off with his legs into the path of an oncoming

blade. His fingers caught the edge and his body slammed into the fibreglass. The wind was knocked out of him and pain shot through his hand. As he struggled to breathe and wrapped his arms and legs round the blade, he felt himself lifted into the air.

The rotating blade swung him upward and then descended again, before it finally ground to a halt.

Jake was suspended, 150 feet above the forest floor.

'Help!' he called out, his legs swinging wildly beneath him. A crowd had gathered below, tiny figures. 'Help!' he shouted again.

He heard a creaking sound from above and looked up. A fine crack had formed where the blade he was hanging from joined the axle of the turbine.

Fear hit him like a punch in the gut.

Jake slithered along and reached for the axle, looping a hand around each side. Just as he did so, the blade sheared away. He watched it crash through the leaves and into the control room roof.

But he wasn't safe yet. The mast and the ladder were five feet away. Jake swung his legs towards the rungs, but he couldn't get close. And with each swing his grip on the huge axle loosened.

Jake looked down desperately, feeling the fire across his

shoulders from the effort of holding himself up. *This is how I'm going to die*, he thought.

'Jake! Just hold on!' shouted a voice.

His dad was scaling the ladder with surprising speed. His limp didn't seem to bother him. 'Hang on, son!' he yelled, his face contorted with the effort of climbing. 'Don't let go!'

Jake's hands slipped, slick with sweat. 'Dad! Hurry!'

His dad came level, panting for breath. His eyes seemed to pass over the scene in a second. With one hand on the rung, the other was scrabbling at his belt. He unfastened the buckle and pulled it free.

'Jake,' he said, 'listen to me carefully. 'I'm going to swing this to you. You need to grab the end.'

'I can't,' said Jake. Desperation clawed at his insides. 'You won't be able to hold me.'

His dad looped the belt once round his own wrist, and looked Jake dead in the eye. 'I won't drop you, Jake.' His voice was calm. 'Ready?'

There was no choice. Jake couldn't hold on much longer. His dad swung the leather belt, buckle-end first, in Jake's direction. Jake released his grip and reached for the belt. One hand closed on the buckle, he swung forward and a millisecond later the other hand grabbed a rung on the ladder. He saw his dad's face in slow motion, clenched against Jake's weight, his eyes pleading for his son to hold on.

Jake slammed into the mast and his feet found the rungs. He sucked in deep breaths and the adrenalin seeped from his veins, leaving him weak as a kitten.

I'm safe! his mind screamed. *I'm alive!*

A great cheer went up from below, whooping and shouting in several languages. Jake closed his eyes and was aware of his dad speaking.

'Time to go down, Jake. Can you climb?'

Jake began the descent unsteadily. His limbs felt like lead but as the ground came nearer he began to recover. A new feeling crept up. Anger.

Dr Dowden was lying on the grass in the recovery position, while Hans and the other scientist were tending to him. For a moment, Jake feared he might be dead, but a slight movement told him otherwise. Truman, Popov and two security guards were standing to one side, and the rest of the team stood further back. Devon Taylor came forward to help Jake from the bottom of the ladder. He bent over to catch his breath and heard the American say, 'That was amazing, Jake. You saved Dr Dowden's life!'

His dad came down shortly behind him. Jake was surprised that he was hardly even sweating. The other footballers murmured praise, stepping forward to pat them both on the back.

Popov was staring up at the turbine, his tongue playing against the inside of his cheek. He looked like he was controlling his emotions – but what emotions? Relief? Fury? Frustration? Dr Dowden groaned softly.

'He needs to go to hospital,' Hans said. 'Hypothermia.'

'Sure,' said Truman. He pointed to one of the security team. 'You there, call an ambulance.'

Jake's dad walked towards him and before Jake knew it he was in a tight embrace. 'I thought I'd lost you, son,' he said. His voice was choked.

Jake remembered Daniel Powell's body plummeting towards the centre circle. He'd almost met the same fate. He couldn't contain his anger, and shoved his dad hard in the chest. His dad stumbled, but didn't go down, much to Jake's annoyance.

Jake pushed past Devon and sprinted into the forest.

'Jake!' his dad shouted, sounding utterly confused. 'Come back here.'

Jake didn't know where he was going. He wanted only one thing: to be away from his dad and all the lies and death and chaos that followed him. There was no track between the trees and the sound of his footsteps was swallowed up by the thick carpet of pine needles. He leapt over fallen trunks and dodged around stumps, his legs working on autopilot while thoughts thundered in his brain. Chernoff. Powell. The two pilots. Now Dowden. Innocent men, all caught up in some deadly game that his dad and Igor Popov were playing. He remembered bitterly how much he'd wanted to come to Russia. How he'd practically begged.

He'd grown up thinking his dad was a footballer. A straightforward defender his team-mates could rely on. Who *he* could rely on. *What a laugh!*

'Jake, stop!' his dad called. The voice was close. Jake risked a glance back and saw his dad charging after him through the trees. Jake pushed on, but he couldn't believe it. His dad was catching him.

What about his limp?

Jake pumped his legs harder and ducked under a low branch. He looked back again, but couldn't see his dad at all.

Something snagged his foot. The ground rose up to meet him, and Jake put out his hands. The smell of the forest floor was heavy as Jake rolled over.

His dad was standing over him, holding out a hand.

'That's enough, Jake.'

'You're quick for a guy with ligament damage,' Jake spat out. 'Or is that a lie too?'

His dad shot a look around, his eyes alive with suspicion. Against the line of his trousers, Jake made out the shape of something concealed near his ankle. The gun . . . it had to be.

'I can explain,' his dad hissed. 'Just keep your voice down.'

Jake laughed grimly. 'Or what?'

'You don't speak to me like that!' snapped his dad. 'D'you hear?'

Jake made his decision. He'd had enough. 'I'm sorry,' he said, grasping for his dad's outstretched hand. With one hand he pulled himself up, but he kicked hard with his foot, raking the edge down his dad's shin – an Olly Price special. His dad cried out and fell backward.

'What the hell!' he shouted.

Jake scrambled on top of him, driving an elbow into his dad's gut. While his dad tried to stand, Jake leant across his legs and tore at the bottom of his trousers. He pulled out the gun and rolled off. His dad sprang up quickly, panic in his eyes.

Jake aimed the gun at his dad's chest. 'I'll speak to you how I want . . . Dad.'

14

Jake wasn't sure what he expected, but his dad didn't raise his hands or cower. He simply stood there, arms at his sides.

'Put the gun down.'

Jake's senses were focused on his finger and the trigger it touched. He tensed. *A tiny twitch, that's all it would take . . . and I'd be a killer, too. Like father, like son.*

'Jake, you don't know what you're doing.'

'This is the second gun I've held this week,' Jake said, failing to keep the tremor out of his voice. 'I know what to do with it.'

'Jake, I'm your father for God's sake. Don't point that thing at me.'

'Not till you tell me what's going on. Why have you got a gun?'

His dad took a step forward. Jake backed off, but kept a

firm grip on the hilt. 'You're a killer, aren't you? Some kind of assassin.'

There were shouts from far off. The others were searching for them.

'It's not like that,' his dad said. 'I carry a weapon for protection.'

Jake snorted and shook his head. 'More lies. Like the fake limp.'

His dad took a heavy breath. 'Jake, there isn't much time. I can explain everything, but you have to give me back the gun and give me a chance.'

'Like you gave Chernoff, you mean? And Powell? You're nothing but a gangster, and you're not going to get away with it.'

'Coach?' Devon yelled from somewhere between the trees. 'Jake?'

'Jake,' said his dad, looking him dead in the eye. 'Yes, I've lied to you. I've lied to you all your life. But now I'm telling you the truth.' He cast a furtive glance behind him, then spoke quickly in a low voice. 'I work for MI6. Popov is my target – the coaching job's a means to an end. Andy was my informant. I found out after we arrived that Powell was CIA – the Americans are on to Popov too. Andy and Powell died because they knew too much, and I'm damned if that's going to happen to you.'

Jake was speechless.

'I don't believe you.'

Twigs cracked nearby. The others were close.

'If they find us with this gun, it's all over,' his dad said. 'Everything.' He looked serious enough. His words were laced with desperation.

No, it didn't add up.

'What about the fight with Powell?'

'What fight?' His dad's face creased in confusion, which became a frown of anger. 'You've been spying on me?'

'Must run in the family,' said Jake. 'You warned him off.'

'I was worried he was going to blow my cover. Powell was reckless – the CIA have never been good at playing the long game.'

The rustle of footsteps came from nearby. 'I think I've found them,' shouted a voice. 'This way.'

Jake's dad leapt forward. Jake felt a pressure on his wrist and then the gun was gone. His dad released and concealed it in a single movement. He placed an arm over Jake's shoulder and turned him round so they were side by side.

Christian Truman stepped out of the trees with Devon and Popov. The Texan was wearing a worried grin, and took off his hat to fan his face. 'Say, you guys all right?'

Jake's dad pasted a smile on his own mouth and wheeled to face the others. 'Sure, Christian. Just a dad–son dispute. Nothing serious, you know.'

'Yessir, I surely do,' replied the American.

Popov cut in. 'Steven, an ambulance is on its way for Dr Dowden. I want Jake to go as well. That's a nasty cut on his hand.'

Jake only now noticed it. He must have opened the graze from the motorbike crash. Blood was dripping steadily on to the forest floor.

With a last look at his dad, he followed the others back towards the house.

Jake and his dad climbed into the ambulance while Dr Dowden was receiving treatment on a stretcher. As they pulled away from the ranch, the paramedics stabilised Dr Dowden using heated blankets and injecting fluids intravenously. Jake was given a compress to stop the bleeding.

'Will he be all right?' Jake asked.

'He should be,' his dad said.

The doctor's face was pale and lifeless at first, but the blue colouring in his lips gradually faded. By the time they reached the private hospital on the edge of the city, he'd recovered the power of speech.

He reached weakly from under his blanket and touched Jake's arm. 'Thank you,' he croaked. 'You saved my life.'

'You're welcome,' Jake said.

As the doctor was wheeled to a ward for monitoring, Jake and his dad were led to a treatment room. A nurse cleaned Jake's wound. While he worked, neither Jake nor his dad spoke.

'I go bring somebody for stitching,' said the nurse in broken English.

As the door closed behind him, Jake spoke up. 'Why should I believe you?'

His dad was silent for several seconds, then put his hand on Jake's shoulder. 'Because I'm your dad. And I would never do anything to harm you.'

Jake resisted the urge to shrug off the hand. He thought back to all the sneaking around and spying he'd done since they came to Russia, and even before that, in London. And his dad had done his best not to bring Jake with him. The only reason he had was because Jake had played on his sense of guilt.

'It's the truth, Jake. You have to trust me.'

Jake remembered the pain on his dad's face when Andrew Chernoff had died in front of them. He remembered the fear he'd shown when he raced up the turbine ladder.

There was nothing false there. But MI6! A secret agent? It was too much to take in.

His dad slid his hand off Jake's shoulder and held it out. 'No more secrets.'

Jake looked at his dad's face. The emotion in his eyes wasn't like anything he'd seen before. It wasn't the look a dad gave his son. It was an unblinking stare that said 'trust me'.

He took the hand and squeezed. 'No more secrets.'

After Jake's hand was stitched up and he was released, his dad asked about Dr Dowden in the hospital reception. He was told the doctor was recovering on the third floor, and that he was allowed visitors. As they climbed into the lift together, Jake's mind focused again on the incident in the wind turbine. It was definitely foul play. But who stood to gain from Dr Dowden's death? Was someone trying to sabotage Christian Truman's renewable energy initiatives?

The pen-drive. Hector Elisandos. Two scientists linked to Truman. One missing, the other almost killed. Suddenly Jake was flooded with guilt. Powell was handing information to another agent, his equivalent in MI6. He, Jake, had got in the way.

What have I done?

He was about to say something when the doors pinged

open on the third floor.

They stepped out and a tall nurse brushed past into the elevator. Jake's nostrils caught the ghost of her perfume lingering on the air. His eyes stung and he coughed to clear his throat.

Strong perfume. Just like when . . .

Jake spun on his heels as the lift doors were closing. It was only for a split second, but he saw the nurse's face clearly enough: pale skin, blue eyes, a plump lower lip.

It was a face he'd last seen leaping from a burning aeroplane at something close to 10,000 feet.

Helga.

'What's wrong, Jake?' his dad said.

'It's the flight attendant from the plane crash,' he mumbled. 'We've got to get to Dowden!'

Jake ran towards the wards, with his dad close behind. He heard the panic before he rounded the next corner. Doctors and nurses speaking urgently. The squeal of wheels on the linoleum floor. Electronic whining.

It's a flatline.

Half a dozen medical staff surrounded the bed. One was greasing a defibrillator while a nurse pulled a hospital garment aside to reveal Dr Dowden's chest. A doctor shouted and everyone made space. The paddles were placed on Dr Dowden's chest and his body arched as the current was applied. Jake saw the flat green line on the monitor arc, then fall back to horizontal. The doctors repeated the procedure with the same effect.

He's gone . . .

After the third attempt, the doctor with the paddles shook his head. He spoke a few words in Russian, which Jake recognised as the time. A nurse scribbled it on Dr Dowden's chart.

The time of death.

15

Jake's dad hurried them out of the hospital by the stairs and into the car park. They took a taxi back to the house. Jake noticed his dad eyeing the driver suspiciously, and took the hint not to speak. He found he was shaking, but not with fear: with anger. He'd saved Dr Dowden the first time; the second he'd arrived perhaps half a minute too late.

At the house, his dad paid the driver and went straight through to his son's bedroom. Jake followed. His dad pulled out a suitcase from under the bed and immediately began throwing clothes into it. His mouth was set in a grim, determined line.

'Dad, what are you doing?'

'It's not safe for you here any more, Jake,' he said, stuffing Jake's jeans into the case. 'I can't protect you. It's time to go.'

Jake grabbed the lid of the case and closed it.

'What are you talking about?' he protested. 'I can't go now.'

'Wrong,' his dad said. 'You'll be on the next flight to Milan.' He yanked the wardrobe door open and began taking the shirts off the hangers.

'Dad, wait,' said Jake. 'You need me here. Another pair of eyes.'

'Wrong again,' said his dad. 'Dr Dowden was murdered. You almost died. This isn't a game. Damn it! I *knew* I shouldn't have let you come.'

There was no room for compromise in his dad's voice. Jake had to think fast.

'I think I know what's going on,' he said. 'I think Popov's behind it.'

His dad shook his head. 'Tell me something I don't know.'

Jake swallowed. 'Have you heard the name Hector Elisandos?'

His dad stopped the frenzied packing and looked up.

'No. What's he got to do with all this?'

Jake's heart was thumping as he told his dad about the pen-drive. About seeing Powell place it in his jacket pocket. About the article. He went over and took the small pen-drive out of the toe of his football boot. His dad stared at it in bewilderment, then held out his hand.

'You stole from me?' his dad said.

'I thought you were a criminal,' Jake replied, handing

it over. 'I'm really sorry.'

His dad's face was flushed with anger, and Jake could see the emotions fighting inside him.

'Do you realise what you've done?' he said quietly. 'If I'd known this, I could have looked out for Dr Dowden. He might still be alive.'

Jake felt a huge wave of shame wash over him. He couldn't think of anything to say apart from 'I'm sorry' again.

His dad walked out of the room and shut the door behind him.

Jake sat on the bed and put his head in his hands. He'd messed up. Big time.

It was about twenty minutes later when his dad knocked on the door again. Jake asked him to come in, and watched him walk stiffly over to the window.

'Jake, about before,' his dad said, sitting beside him. 'It was my fault. If I hadn't kept so many secrets from you, this never would have happened. Dr Dowden's dead because of *me* – not you.'

It was big of his dad to apologise, but Jake wasn't going to let him take the blame.

'Dr Dowden's dead because of Popov,' he said. 'He ordered that woman to kill him, I know he did.' Jake looked towards his half-packed case. 'Listen, Dad, why not let me stay at least for the game tomorrow? If you send me back now, it'll only raise suspicions. Nothing can happen in the next day or so, can it? There'll be eighty thousand people watching.'

His dad hesitated. 'All right. But after tomorrow, that's it. Understood?'

Jake tried not to let his jubilation show. 'Understood.' As his dad stood up to leave, he added: 'Anyway, it's nearly nine. I can't leave in the middle of the night.'

His dad paused, hand on the doorframe. 'Son, MI6 could get you to Antarctica tonight if they really wanted to. Sleep well.'

Jake woke the next day aching all over, but alert. Over breakfast, he and his dad discussed plans. If anything looked wrong at the ground Jake was to let his dad know immediately.

'I want to know where you are at all times,' he said sternly. 'You do *nothing* without telling me first. Got it?'

Jake nodded. 'Do you think it'll be OK today?'

'I hope so,' his dad said. 'Popov would be crazy to try anything. He's got too much to lose.'

They left the house just after one o'clock, and were running late by the time they arrived at the stadium forty minutes later. It was a glorious day, without a cloud in sight. The programme sellers and fast-food stands had already set up outside, and fans were streaming into the ground.

'Perfect football weather . . .' said his dad wistfully. For a fleeting moment, Jake wondered just how much he missed playing.

The driver took a private approach road. They reached the northern side of the stadium and found a temporary stage that had been set up in the VIP car park. Above them, the last bits of scaffolding had been removed, revealing a large rectangle of material suspended over the top part of the stadium wall, covering something. Ropes dangled either side and were tied off behind the stage. His dad explained that Christian Truman was supposed to be making a big announcement outside the stadium before the game.

A crowd had gathered around the stage. There were even more journalists than at the press conference two days before, as well as plenty of men in flash suits with glamorously-dressed wives and girlfriends. Christian Truman was standing with Igor Popov beside a podium at one end. Jake's dad handed him a pass. 'This is your ticket. Access all areas. You best get out of the car here.'

'What about you?' Jake asked. 'Don't you want to hear the speech?'

His dad checked his watch. 'No time. I have to go and prep the team.'

As Jake popped the door, his dad leant across and made a fist. Just like he used to do when he came off the bench in big games. 'Be careful, son,' he said. 'And stay –'

Jake smiled as they bumped knuckles. 'I know, out of trouble.'

He shut the door and watched the car descend the ramp to the underground car park. He turned his attention to the stage. Igor Popov spotted him from the podium and gave a nod of acknowledgement. Jake had never liked him, but now he was one hundred per cent sure he was staring into the eyes of a cold-blooded killer. He waved back as naturally as possible.

Christian Truman approached the microphone and gave it a couple of taps. The sound reverberated through the speakers. 'Ladies and Gentlemen, it's an honour to be here today at the inaugural match of this magnificent new stadium. Truman Oil has always been a big supporter of sports, and soccer especially represents many of the values dear to my company: teamwork, trust, determination.'

And money, thought Jake.

'But there's more to it than that,' said Truman. 'Soccer represents the future too. Bringing people from all over the world together. This match will be watched on international satellite networks, from Austin, Texas, to Sydney, Australia. From Chile to China. More than ever we live in a global community.

The world doesn't belong to one company, or one country; it's shared by all of us. And we need to look after it.'

Here it comes, thought Jake.

'Our vital resources won't last forever. Maybe not this year or the next, but slowly, steadily, the oil and natural gas our planet has stored over millions of years will run out. That's why I'm here to announce that I'm closing down Truman Oil.' He paused, letting the murmur of surprise spread across the crowd. 'As of today, we have a new venture. Ladies and Gentlemen, I give you . . . *Truman Energy*!'

On the outer wall of the north stand the great sheet dropped away, revealing a huge logo. Two letters – a T and an E – painted green and interlocked inside a circle. The symbolism was crude, but effective. Green technology.

The crowd applauded for a few seconds and cameras clicked away at the display. Jake supposed it had to be a good thing if a man as wealthy as Christian Truman was willing to change course so dramatically for the sake of the planet.

'It won't be easy,' said the American. 'There will be opposition. But together, we can get across the message that change is possible. That's why, over the past two years, I've been working with the greatest scientific minds in their respective fields. Together they form the AEB, the "Alternative Energy Board".' He paused and nodded towards the edge

167

of the stage. Two women and a man climbed the steps and stood beside him, looking slightly uncomfortable in the limelight. 'May I introduce Dr Farrah Evans, leading expert in the use of biofuels, from Cambridge University; Professor Nakata Rei, whose papers on geothermal energy have made her famous in Japan and across the globe; and last, but not least, Dr Sebastian Groeber, whose work with solar panels has revolutionised the way we gather energy from the sun.'

The crowd applauded again and the scientists clapped too, bobbing their heads in acknowledgement. Rei was probably in her late thirties, while Evans and Groeber were significantly older, both with grey hair.

Truman held up a hand to curtail the applause. He wore a sombre look. 'Sadly, this is also a day of mourning. Two people can't be with us. I had planned for the AEB to be a meeting of five great minds. But Hector Elisandos, the world's authority on tidal energy, is still missing. We hope he is found safe as soon as possible. And as you may have heard, another of our partners, Dr Ian Dowden, passed away yesterday as the result of a freak accident.' Truman's voice became choked with emotion. 'I worked closely with Ian, and he was a dear friend. He was looking forward to today even more than me. So it's to him that I'd like to dedicate this celebration.' He left a moment's pause.

If only you knew, thought Jake. *Popov killed both of them. So much for East and West as one world.*

'There will be a minute's silence at the start of the match, when the AEB members and myself will gather in the centre circle with the players,' Truman continued. 'I call on all fans of soccer to respect it. Please, I hope you all enjoy the magnificent game we have planned today.'

Jake joined in the clapping as Truman and the scientists climbed down the steps. But from the corner of his eyes he saw Igor Popov and four of his hulking security men. He was whispering to them and pointing in various directions. They all nodded menacingly.

Five scientists. One definitely dead. Another almost certainly floating in the Caribbean Sea. Now the other three, the key to the AEB and to Truman Energy, were gathered in one place.

Like ducks in a barrel, Jake thought.

Of course! That's what Powell had been trying to tell his dad. That the AEB were *all* in danger. That *someone* was willing to kill to stop Christian Truman's vision of worldwide green energy becoming a reality. Someone who had a fortune invested in oil and a willingness to do anything to protect that monopoly. Someone exactly like Igor Popov.

They're all walking into a trap.

16

Jake had to show his pass four times between the gates and the changing room. The chanting of the crowd sounded through the stadium like a distant thunderstorm. He ran along the corridor and found his dad sharing a joke with the match referee and linesmen outside his office.

'Dad,' he said. 'I need to talk to you.'

'In a minute,' his dad said. He shook hands with the officials and turned to his son. 'OK, Jake, make it quick. I need to give a team talk to the players. They'll be back from the warm–up any minute.'

'We have to warn Truman and the AEB,' he said. 'They're in danger.'

His dad grabbed his arm and swung Jake into the office with him. He shut the door. 'Jake, keep your voice down,' he hissed. 'Popov's got people everywhere.'

'Yes, I know . . . and they're going to kill the other scientists.'

'The alternate energy lot? No way. Not here. There are thousands of people watching.'

'But what if he makes it look like an accident?'

His dad put a hand on both shoulders. 'Jake, leave this to me. I've been doing this a long time. People like Popov, they're criminals, but they're not stupid.'

'But what about Elisandos and Dowden?'

The sound of football boots clattered along the tunnel outside and someone knocked, then stuck his head round the door. It was Devon, with the rest of the team streaming past behind him, all sweating from the warm-up. 'Hey, coach,' said Devon, grinning. 'You coming to put the fear of God into us?'

'I'll be there in a minute,' said Jake's dad. He closed the door and turned back to Jake. 'The AEB will be perfectly safe in the VIP box. I heard Truman's watching the game from Popov's office – he'll be on the phone to his US partners, I guess. There's going to be a big dinner afterwards in the restaurant. No one's going to get hurt today – Popov wouldn't take that risk. Not with the media attention . . .'

'Ten minutes, Mr Bastin!' shouted a voice from the end of the tunnel.

'Look, I have to go, Jake. Relax. Enjoy the game.'

171

His dad left him standing in the corridor.

But Jake couldn't relax. *He's wrong. I know he is.* He felt helpless. But who could he tell? Not the security teams. They all worked for Popov. There was only one person who could help: Christian Truman. He could step up security for himself and the AEB.

Jake sprinted to the elevators and punched the button for the third floor. The lift was full of well-dressed table staff moving supplies up to the restaurant. He almost collided with an attractive waitress carrying a tray of glasses filled with bubbling champagne. As the lift ascended he was plagued by doubts. What would his dad say if he found out what Jake was doing? He'd been so angry with Powell when he risked blowing their cover. Wasn't Jake doing the same thing now?

But Jake wasn't going to sit back and let more innocent people die. Not like Dr Dowden.

When the lift doors opened he found the office-like space he had been in a few days before. Only now it was teeming with activity. Behind the glass partitions workers tapped away at keyboards and babbled into headphones. The whole operations team behind the broadcasting and organisation of the game going on below. No one batted an eyelid at the boy hurrying along the corridor. A security guard stood at the end of the passage leading to Popov's office. He placed his bulk in the centre of the carpet.

'Can I help you?' he said in an American accent.

'I need to see Mr Truman,' replied Jake.

'He doesn't want to be disturbed,' said the man. His voice and body language left little room to negotiate.

'Can you at least tell him Jake Bastin is here to see him? I'm the coach's son.' He flashed his pass. 'It's an emergency.'

The security guard stared at the card. 'Wait here,' he said.

He lumbered off towards the door, knocked twice, then entered. A few seconds later he re-emerged, his face impassive.

'Mr Truman will see you,' said the guard, stepping aside.

Jake squeezed past and hurried into the office. Christian Truman was sitting in Popov's leather chair, a cigar fixed in his jaws. 'Hey, Jake, shut the door. What can I do for you?'

Jake started speaking before the door clicked shut. 'Mr Truman, I think the AEB scientists are in danger. I think someone is going to kill them –'

'Whoa!' Truman interrupted, taking out his cigar. 'Steady on there, kid. What do you mean?'

Behind him, Jake could see the stadium alive with flags and banners. Muted cheering penetrated the thick glass viewing panel of the office.

Jake tried to explain, without blowing his father's cover, but it was hard. Almost impossible. Truman wore a patient smile as Jake came to the end of his reasoning.

'Kid, Dr Dowden was a freak accident,' he replied. 'A tragedy, yes. Unusual, yes. But he wasn't killed. The doctors said he died from a hypothermic reaction.'

'But what about Hector Elisandos?'

'Missing,' said Truman. 'But he isn't dead. He's probably on the run from the tax officials, for all I know. These South Americans. They're great fun, but the politics down there . . .' He shook his head, as if that finished his sentence.

'Aren't you listening?' said Jake. 'Powell, the journalist, he died too.'

'Yes, he did,' said Truman. 'But the papers in the States are saying he went through a bad divorce. Lost custody of his kids. It's awful when that happens, but it can drive people to do desperate things. Sometimes suicide seems like the only way out.'

It was like talking to a brick wall. 'Mr Truman, I really think you should at least be concerned.'

Truman half turned and gestured out on to the pitch. 'Jake, this is a massive day, not just for Truman Oil – I mean Truman Energy – but also for our relationships with the former Eastern Bloc. I'm not going to cancel anything.'

Jake didn't know what else he could do, or say. Unless . . .

'It's not just me,' said Jake. 'My dad's worried, too.'

Truman took a very deep breath and shook his head in what looked like dismay.

Now he's taking it seriously, Jake thought.

'You spoke to your dad about this?'

Jake nodded eagerly. 'Yeah. He sent me.' The lie tripped out easily. 'He couldn't come himself because he had to stay with the players.'

'OK, Jake. OK. Let me handle this . . .'

As he spoke the words, Jake's mouth went dry. Truman opened his desk drawer and even before he raised his hand, Jake knew what he would be holding.

A gun.

As Jake stood still. Truman's thumb jabbed a button on the desk intercom. 'This is Truman. We've been compromised. Steve Bastin needs to be . . . *relieved* of his position.'

17

Jake had seen this scene in the movies a thousand times, but that was nothing compared to the reality of staring down at the barrel of a gun. Fear spread like cold fire over his skin. He wanted to run, to warn his father, but there was nowhere for him to go. The gun seemed to pin him to the spot.

'I'm sorry, Jake,' said Truman. His gravelly voice had lost all its warmth.

Jake couldn't work it out. 'What . . . I mean . . . What's going on?'

'You couldn't keep your nose out, that's what,' said Truman. 'I tried to give you an out. I tried to be a good guy. But you wouldn't let me . . . You just had to keep on meddling. Well, you've kicked your last soccer ball, kid.'

'It was you all along,' said Jake. His eyes darted over the office, looking for something to use as a weapon. Nothing.

Truman chuckled. 'I'm afraid I can't take all the credit, Jake. I don't like to get my own hands too dirty, so I pay professionals for the nasty stuff.'

'Dr Dowden?' said Jake.

'And Elisandos,' replied Truman. 'Once he was in the water bleeding, I heard the sharks did the rest.'

Jake shivered inwardly. 'But why? You need those guys. Without their expertise Truman Energy will fail.'

'And that's exactly what I want it to do.' Truman grinned. 'Have you any idea how much money the international community is willing to donate to renewable energy initiatives like mine? Billions. Governments all over the world, the US especially, have found ways to get round the carbon targets, or straight-up ignore them. All I have to do is a good job of *acting* like I give a damn, and I get money thrown at me. It's simple and brilliant.'

Now Jake understood. 'So you get all the cash, but don't deliver the goods.'

Truman laughed loud, deep from his belly, and the gun wobbled off target. Jake backed up slightly, but Truman snapped the barrel back on to him.

'Bingo,' said Truman. 'When a Texan comes along and says he wants to change − really *change* − well, let's just say, they've been falling over their feet to give me their dollars.'

It all made sense. 'You're like a parasite,' said Jake. 'Leeching off good will. You have no intention of delivering on your promises.'

'Of course I don't,' said Truman. 'The future's oil. Always has been. Always will be.'

'The oil is running out,' said Jake. 'It has seventy, a hundred years at most.'

'That's good enough for me and my nearest,' said Truman. 'The winners will be the guys with enough money to find it and exploit it.'

Jake felt sick as he realised the full depravity of Truman's plan. 'So you got the AEB together to show you were serious and get the funding, but you always knew you'd have to kill them.'

'It had to be done,' said Truman. 'Or should I say, it *has* to be done.'

'But the whole world's watching.'

'That's the beauty of it, don't you see? I'm the last person the world will suspect. We're in Russia, for Chrissakes. Sitting on top of enormous oil and gas reserves. There are plenty of people here who'd be only too happy to see the AEB six feet under.'

'Everyone will think it's Popov,' said Jake.

'Just like you did,' laughed Truman. 'If you think I'm slimy, get a load of this guy. He'd sell his own grandma if he thought he could make a profit. He's the perfect scapegoat.'

Jake couldn't see a flaw. *Everyone* would suspect Popov. The dodgy businessman, the Russian oligarch, the guy with so much to lose. Truman could leak stories to the American press, make sure the right evidence reached the right desks, and . . .

'Popov will be public enemy number one,' he murmured.

'Not just in Russia, but the entire world,' said Truman proudly.

Truman leant down to the drawer again and took out what Jake thought was a cigar case. Only when Truman began screwing it into the barrel of the gun did he realise what it actually was. A silencer. He was running out of time.

'You won't get away with it, you know,' said Jake. His fear had gone, replaced with anger. 'People like you always get caught. Other people know about this.'

'What, like Daniel Powell?' said Truman. 'I thought I'd taken care of that little bastard on the flight over. Didn't know your old man could fly planes.' Truman laughed. 'He's really something, huh?' The Texan gestured with the gun. 'Now turn round and put your hands up.'

Jake did as he was told, slowly. He was facing the cabinet lined with photos and trophies. Maybe he could use one as a weapon. He eyed the centrepiece of the display: a huge trophy with a metal football on a silver stand.

No real match for a gun.

Through the office window Jake could see the digital clock set high in the stadium, counting down to the inaugural match. Just over a minute left.

'My dad knows I'm here,' he said.

He could hear Truman's movements as he walked out from the other side of the desk. In the reflection of one of the photo frames, he saw the American position himself behind him.

'What makes you think your dad's still alive?'

Truman levelled the gun at his head.

Now or never.

Jake ducked and drove an elbow into Truman's groin. The gun gave a soft *pfft*, and Jake heard the bullet ricochet off a surface. He grabbed the trophy with his right hand and twisted, swinging it at Truman's head just as he brought the barrel round for another shot. The metal football came loose from the trophy and thudded into Truman's cheekbone. He staggered backward, flailing his arms. Jake turned the trophy stand in his hand and swung again, this time hitting Truman's chin. Another *pfft* sounded as Truman span round. He crumpled on to the floor, his mouth hanging open. Out cold.

Jake looked around, breathing heavily. The first bullet had embedded in the wall, the second in the glass viewing panel, sending out a web of cracks in all directions.

That could have been my head. Once again he'd been only inches from death.

The gun was still in Truman's limp hand. Jake kicked it away.

There was a huge roar from the stands and Jake rushed to the viewing window. It was directly opposite the coaches' dugouts, and he could see both the Tigers and their opposition, the All-Stars, running out on to the pitch. There was nothing in the players' faces to suggest anything was wrong.

And there, following the team out, was his dad. He was waving to the crowd. He was safe, for now.

The teams formed two lines as the announcer introduced the day's special guests: the remaining members of the AEB. As the three scientists took the field, the announcer said there'd be a minute's silence for their deceased colleague, Dr Ian Dowden.

Jake held his breath. Camera flashes went off all over the stadium. Jake flinched. It would only take one to be the glint from a rifle sight. But the minute ended and the players broke from the centre circle and ran to to their respective halves. The AEB members were escorted off the pitch.

Truman had given the order to 'relieve' Jake's dad of his position. It did not mean that he was getting the sack – it meant that he was marked for death. But Jake knew that the AEB were in danger too. He had a choice.

My dad or the scientists?

18

Truman groaned on the carpet. Jake rushed to the side of the desk and picked up the gun, but Truman wasn't moving. Jake thought about taking the weapon with him, but it was too big a risk. He inspected the mechanism and flicked the release switch. The clip dropped out. Jake pocketed it and took the gun through the side door into a small bathroom area. He dropped it into the toilet. Even if Truman had another clip, the wet gun would be useless.

Jake headed back to the main office door and slipped through as Truman shifted a fraction on the floor, still moaning softly. The security guard was standing at the end of the corridor, oblivious. Jake walked as calmly as possible past him and back along the corridor towards the lift. He didn't look round until he stepped into the elevator. The security guard hadn't moved.

As the lift descended, Jake's mind was doing calculations.

It would take a good five minutes to reach his dad on the other side of the stadium. Perhaps two and a half to get to the spectator box where the AEB would be watching.

What would my dad do?

His dad was at the pitch side, surrounded by journalists and the public. The AEB were on their own, or perhaps chaperoned by Truman's men. His dad knew how to look after himself, but the scientists had no idea what they were involved in. Jake made his decision.

But how could he get to the VIP box? If Truman was planning to kill the AEB in there it would be heavily guarded by his men. By now, they'd know that his dad, and probably Jake too, were trouble. He probably wouldn't get in through the front door.

Jake exited the lift and headed for the stands, dropping the magazine of bullets into a bin on the way. He walked out through a small tunnel and found himself in one of the corners where the visiting supporters were seated. The game was already in progress and Jake saw the goalkeeper, Emery, launch a long throw to Benalto in midfield.

The VIP box was about fifty yards away and positioned above the main stands. Maybe if he could get below it he could somehow raise the alarm, or climb up. He began to thread his way past grumbling spectators, who had to shift backward to let him pass by. Halfway along, the crowd all stood in unison and let out a collective gasp. Janné was standing with his head in his hands on the pitch, and the ball was in the stands behind. Jake guessed he'd just missed a sitter.

As the crowd took their seats again, Jake spotted one of Truman's security team emerging from an entrance tunnel ahead. He was easy to pick out – huge and dressed in black. He was speaking into a walkie-talkie and scanning the stands with a small pair of binoculars. Jake joined the end of a row of seats, pretending to watch the game. From the corner of his eye, he saw more security emerging across the stands.

It looked like Christian Truman had woken up.

The man next to Jake had left his Tigers scarf and hat draped over the back of his seat. While he sat forward and watched Calas chasing a ball towards the corner flag, Jake casually leant behind him, took the scarf and hat, then stood and headed up for the next tier. He wrapped the scarf around his neck and pulled the hat down as low as he could. Now he blended in with the thousands of spectators.

The VIP box was only about twenty yards away and Jake could make out a couple of shapes through the tinted glass. It made perfect sense. Whatever Truman was planning, no one would see the assassin.

The crowd volume was rising. One of the All-Stars raced down the near wing. Another player was waiting in the centre for a pass that would split the Tigers' defence in two. But Devon Taylor was tracking back with the winger, just a couple of yards behind and gaining. Then he lunged.

The tackle was dreadful. Two-footed, high and from behind. The All-Stars player crashed to the turf, rolling over several times and gripping the back of his knee. Devon stayed down too. The referee sprinted over, reaching for his top pocket. He flourished a red card.

Jake saw his dad shaking his head and talking to the assistant coach. He would be furious. The game was only a friendly – there was no need to tackle like that. What had got into Devon? Had he been watching videos of Roy Keane, or something? Still, though, he didn't get up. The All-Stars player was now limping away, trying to run off the injury.

Security guards were still scouring the stands, and one brushed right past Jake without spotting him. To move now would be a mistake. Everyone else was in their seats watching the drama unfold below.

Stretcher-bearers had rushed across the field for Devon. It looked like he'd paid a high price for his dangerous tackle.

Taylor was helped on to the stretcher and carried off the

pitch. Jake watched his dad give the stricken player a pat on the shoulder and share a few words, before Devon was taken down the tunnel.

The game settled down again and Jake waited to make his move. It came when the Tigers won a free kick, twenty-five yards out.

Just the kind of distance we were practising the other day, Jake thought. But didn't *that* feel like a long time ago?

Benalto stood over the ball as the wall assembled. The crowd hushed.

He ran up, looking to blast it, but instead kicked it with the outside of his boot, square to Lee Po Heng. The defenders and the keeper were completely wrong-footed and the Korean slid the ball neatly along the ground inside the far post. The crowd erupted as Heng lifted both arms and ran towards the dugout in celebration.

One-nil to the Tigers.

Jake took his chance and moved back towards one of the empty exit passages near the VIP box. He got as far as the end of the passage, before a hand landed on his shoulder.

'Can I help you?' said the security guard in his native language.

Jake shook his head and pointed to the lavatories. He said 'toilet' in Russian.

But the guard was peering at him more closely now and asked to see his ticket.

Reluctantly, Jake pulled out his pass. The guard took one look at the name and gave an ugly smile. He stepped forward and pushed the hat off Jake's head. 'Hello, Englishman,' he said. 'You are coming with me.'

Behind them, the holding area they were in was completely empty. No one was watching. The guard was only Jake's height, but probably four stone heavier.

Jake turned to look over his shoulder, but it was just a ruse to give him extra power. As he whipped back round, he brought up his right fist and planted it straight into the guard's jaw. He hit the sweet spot and the Russian's head snapped sideways. He staggered towards the wall, but he was already unconscious as he slid down it. Jake flexed his knuckles, feeling like he might not be able to make a fist again for a few weeks.

It wouldn't be long before the guy was discovered missing. One unanswered call on the walkie-talkie would see to that. Jake managed to get his hands under the guard's armpits and heaved him towards the toilets. He dragged him, back straining, into one of the cubicles. He leant the man's head against the toilet bowl.

There was a crackle of radio static from the guard's jacket.

Jake took out the receiver, which was only the size of a cigarette box, and put it in his back pocket. That way Jake would have an idea when his pursuers were on to him.

Finally, he tucked the guard's knees up towards his chin, and closed the cubicle door. With any luck, no one would find him until half-time.

Jake padded back out into the holding area. It was all clear.

There was a door marked 'Private' halfway along, with an electronic keypad to gain access. By Jake's calculation, the door would lead to an area directly beneath the VIP box. He tried pushing it, but it didn't budge. Taking a step back, he lunged with a kick. He only succeeded in jarring his knee.

There has to be another way.

Suddenly, he heard footsteps coming from the left and backed away, moving towards one of the spectator tunnels. He pressed himself up against the wall and peered out. It wasn't a security guard. A man wearing a hooded top and carrying what looked like a boot-bag was jogging along the holding area. Training staff perhaps. When he reached the private door, he stopped and tapped in a code. There was a tiny electronic beep and he went through. The door began to swing shut behind him.

Jake left his position and sprinted to the door. He slid on to his backside as though stretching to get a toe to a football, and managed to slip the end of his shoe into the gap in the closing door. He stood up, careful to keep it open with his foot, then placed his eye to the crack.

The room looked to be some kind of maintenance area. There were exposed pipes and fuse boxes against the far wall. The hooded figure was clambering on a pile of cardboard boxes.

What's he up to?

The man stood up and removed one of the panels from the ceiling, and laid it carefully beside his feet. He then unzipped the boot-bag and pulled out what looked like a smaller shoebox, with a single LED display. Jake swallowed. There was no doubt in his mind.

It was a bomb.

The man flicked a switch, and placed the device into the ceiling space. Jake stepped into the room.

'What are you doing?'

The figure jerked round.

Jake saw his face and gasped.

It didn't make any sense at all.

Devon Taylor.

19

'You?' said Jake. His legs felt weak. Devon was a footballer, not a terrorist.

'Jake?' said Devon. 'What are you doing here?' He jumped down from the cardboard boxes, landing nimbly. 'I got lost. This place is a maze, isn't . . .?'

'What happened to your injury?' Jake interrupted.

'It was nothing.' Devon smiled. 'I messed up with the tackle though. The ref had no choice . . .'

'You did it on purpose,' said Jake, his mouth just about keeping pace with his brain. What he was saying barely made sense to him, but at the same time he knew it to be true. 'You got yourself sent off so that you could come here and finish the job.'

A cloud passed over Devon's face, wiping away his smile. 'I don't know what you're talking about.'

'You're trying to kill the scientists upstairs,' Jake snarled.

'Well, I'm not letting you. You're not going to get away with this, Devon.'

Devon calmly zipped up the boot-bag. 'You have no choice,' he said. 'As soon as I set the remote detonator,' he tapped his pocket, 'it's a straight countdown to the big bang. The detonation can't be stopped. Oh, don't worry, the blast will be isolated to the VIP box and everyone in it. The bomb is sensitive to touch too, so I wouldn't try anything. If you did . . . well, let's just say your playing days would be over.'

'Why are you doing this?' asked Jake. He was buying time, but his gut seemed to tingle with the need to know just why a superstar footballer was going to murder three scientists. 'I mean . . . what's in it for you?'

Devon grinned. 'Don't play cute with me. What do you think?'

'Money?' said Jake. 'You'd kill innocent people to get rich?'

'Hey, Jake,' said Devon shrugging. 'Look around you. This stadium, the star players. Football *is* money!'

'But you already earn millions,' said Jake. 'You've got the world at your feet.'

Devon fished in his pocket and pulled out something like a small remote control. The detonator.

'Don't you see, Jake? I can still have the glittering football career. But I could have *billions* if my father and I keep Truman Oil at the top.'

Jake didn't get it. 'Your *father*?'

'I'm surprised no one's seen the resemblance,' said Devon. 'True, mom was a model – Annalise Taylor – so perhaps that's where I get my looks from.'

'Christian Truman . . . he's your father?'

'The name can open doors, but I prefer to get where I am on merit.' Devon was fiddling with the timer. 'Ten minutes should be about right, d'you agree?'

Jake lunged for the detonator, but Devon was quicker and snatched it away. Jake felt the footballer's muscled knee slam into his stomach, and fell into a crouch. His breath wouldn't come. Devon sent another kick into his ribs, and Jack smashed into the stacked boxes.

Devon was crouched beside a toolbox, and pulled out a hammer. Jake struggled on to his knees. 'You know, Jake, I actually quite liked you and your dad. It's just a shame you had to get in the way.'

He brought the mallet end of the hammer down in a wide arc. Jake lifted his right arm. The handle caught his wrist and slid off. He drove his left fist into Devon's groin. Devon howled and stumbled backward, bent double. Jake dived after him, ignoring the dull throb in his gut.

Devon was still holding the detonator in his hand. Jake stamped low on to the back of his knee and he screamed in agony. The detonator fell and skidded along the floor, coming to rest against the wall.

As Devon cradled his knee, Jake went after the device. But Devon caught his ankle and brought him down too. He felt his hair yanked back, and then a sharp shove to the back of his head. His face met the floor nose first and white pain took away his vision. He groaned and rolled over. He felt blood oozing over his top lip, its iron tang filling his mouth.

Jake gagged and spat out his own blood. As his vision cleared he saw Devon standing with the detonator. Jake tried to stand, but couldn't.

Devon turned a final switch on the timer. Jake heard a corresponding beep from the bomb lodged in the ceiling. 'See you, Bastin,' said Devon. He pressed the door release button and was gone.

Jake clambered slowly to his feet. Blood spattered from his nose on to the floor, and he squeezed below the bridge to stop the flow. It didn't feel broken. He walked as quickly as possible to the boxes and climbed up. The bomb was emitting a low beep every ten seconds or so, and through his watering eyes Jake saw the digital display read 9.36, counting down at second intervals.

He thought about moving it, but what if Devon was telling the truth and it was touch sensitive? Not only would he kill himself, but the AEB would die anyway. No, there was only one other way. He'd have to find a way to warn them.

9.13.

Jake jumped down, fighting the nausea that made his head swim. Pain would have to wait.

He left the maintenance room and ran out of the holding area and into the lobby. There was a lift at the far end of the tiled reception and the only people there were a business-man wearing a suit and two receptionists. One woman looked at Jake in surprise as he came through. The front of his sweatshirt was covered in blood. She asked if he was OK, but he ignored her, heading straight for the stairs, which were labelled 2a. He ran through the door and up two flights.

He reached the second floor where the VIP box was situated and opened the door. His heart sank. Two security guards were standing either side of the door. Jake knew he didn't stand a chance in a two-on-one situation with guys their size.

If only I'd kept the gun!

Then he remembered the one weapon he did have. He patted his back pocket and found the radio. It seemed a simple enough device: an off/on switch and a button to transmit.

He held down the button and spoke in his best Texan accent.

'All guards in the vicinity. This is Truman. Jake Bastin is coming up stairwell 2b. Take him out. That's Jake Bastin heading to the VIP box on 2b. Over.'

He watched as the two doormen heard the message, shared a few words, then ran in the opposite direction. Jake darted out from his stairwell and made for the VIP area, pulling off his blood-stained sweatshirt as he ran.

Inside, it wasn't like he expected at all. There were close to two dozen people milling around and watching the game below. A waitress was carrying a tray of champagne glasses. At the back of the room, a buffet was laid out on a candlelit table. He spotted Farrah Evans and Sebastian Groeber laughing together.

How long was left on the timer? He had no idea, but it had to be less than five minutes. He imagined the deadly device ticking away just a few feet below. The murmur of raised voices came from the other side of the door. The guards were back. Jake crept across the back of the room and slipped underneath the tablecloth. The door opened and he saw the feet of one of Truman's henchmen, encased in massive steel toecap boots.

The man padded across the carpet, presumably carrying out a quick search, then spoke into his radio.

'No. He's not here. I don't get it. Are you saying that wasn't you?'

He left the room again.

What now? Jake thought about yelling *bomb!* but he knew the security would insist it was a false alarm. He'd have to force the people to leave. But how?

He peeked out from his hiding place and his eyes fell on the candles. There was nothing like a fire to get people running. He snatched one of the sticks and brought the flame under the dangling edges of the tablecloth. It caught quickly. He did the same further along. Then again. Soon the flames were climbing higher and the walls were beginning to scorch black along the back of the table. Jake crawled out.

'Champagne, sir?' asked the waitress, wearing a confused expression. 'Are you all right, sir? You're bleeding.' Her nose twitched, then her eyes widened. 'Oh my God! Fire!'

Her cries drew glances from everyone. Gasps of surprise went around, and a glass smashed as someone dropped it.

'Where's the extinguisher?' someone shouted in panic. The flames suddenly flared higher. A woman screamed.

Jake spotted an extinguisher against the wall and rushed over. He released the mechanism and pretended to squeeze the trigger. 'It's not working!' he said. 'Please, everybody out.'

The door opened and both security guards looked in. 'What's going on? What the hell?'

The first of the VIPs pushed past. 'Are you blind? You have to evacuate people!' he said. 'Everyone follow me!'

As the room filled with smoke, the others started pushing towards the door, moving in a hurried procession along a route furthest from the fire. Jake put down the extinguisher. There couldn't be long left on the timer. 'Hurry up!' he shouted over the crackle of flames.

He coughed into his sleeve as the waitress joined the guards at the back of the line and then went after her, helping to usher the others more quickly.

Outside, he spotted Groeber and Rei together, and rushed up to them.

'Where's Professor Evans?' he asked.

Groeber shook his head. 'She must be here somewhere. She was inside.'

Jake dashed among the assembled VIPs. Evans wasn't there.

She must still be inside!

Jake pushed open the door. The heat inside was intense. Flames licked angrily across the ceiling and smoke swirled like thick fog. He saw patches of the green pitch beyond, which then vanished behind the grey shroud. There was no oxygen at all.

'Professor!' Jake shouted.

A weak moan drew him deeper into the smoke and he saw movement on the far side of the room. It was Farrah Evans. The elderly scientist was lying on the floor, spluttering into her hand.

Jake rushed over and scooped her up. She was a lot lighter than the security guard he'd dragged into the toilet, but the smoke was now so thick he couldn't draw a breath. He couldn't even see the door.

He tripped over a step but managed to stay upright, and with his back against the wall, found the door. In the corridor, panicked faces were gathered at the far end, the security guards amongst them. Jake's head felt heavy and his eyes stung as he stumbled towards them.

Something shoved him hard in the back, lifting his whole body like a powerful wave. *The bomb*. A deafening roar seemed to press his head like a vice, and his eardrums felt ready to burst. It was like being trapped in a tunnel with a freight train thundering past, rattling every bone. The sound and the sensation were one.

Powerless, Jake sprawled forward, spilling Professor Evans on the carpet.

20

Debris filled the corridor and Jake struggled to breathe.

Figures appeared ahead, shadows in the gloom, and then two people were helping Professor Evans off the floor. She looked shaken, but Jake couldn't see any blood.

Another of the VIPs, a woman with red curly hair and spectacles, was crouched in front of him, holding out a hand. Her lips were moving, but Jake couldn't hear anything but the high-pitched ringing in his ears.

'I can't hear you,' he said, pointing to his ears. His own voice sounded like it was being spoken through a microphone.

The woman nodded and helped Jake to his feet. His clothes were covered in dust and something like soot, and he staggered in the direction of the stairs. The rest of the VIPs were gathered there. As he approached, sounds returned to him as though he was hearing them from underwater – distorted voices, the muffled sound of weeping. Then, over all of this, the fire alarm going off, insistent and blaring. Jake gritted his teeth, feeling a mixture of anxiety and sheer frustration: he had saved the scientists' lives, but they were still very much in danger.

'You all need to get out of the stadium,' he said. 'It's not safe here. Take the stairs to the lobby and out into the car park.'

'Who are you?' said one man. 'And what just happened? Was that a bomb?'

'There isn't time to explain,' said Jake. 'Just go.'

To his relief, the crowd seemed to listen and began to file on to the stairs, leaning against each other or holding hands, glancing anxiously around. Jake followed them. *I need to find my dad.* The reception area was already bustling with worried-looking staff, and fans were streaming through from the holding areas, pale-faced and anxious. Orderlies were pointing them in the direction of the main doors. Jake went against the flow, nudging through. When he reached the door to the area behind the stands, a member of staff put his hand across Jake's chest and said in Russian: 'You have to leave. There's a fire.'

'I left my bag in there,' said Jake, then immediately cursed himself for such a lame excuse.

'We're evacuating,' the man said, without any emotion or expression.

'OK,' said Jake, backing away.

But as soon as the man turned his attention elsewhere, Jake ploughed into him.

'Stop!' the man said. Jake was already pushing on through the flow of people. He got through to the holding area, which was thronged with supporters jostling for the exits. Parents were holding on to their children's hands, and people who'd fallen were being helped to their feet. Jake made for the nearest tunnel and elbowed his way into the stands.

A voice sounded over the tannoy, first in Russian. He guessed roughly what was being said before the English translation followed: 'Please remain calm. Make your way to the exits in an orderly manner.'

The voice was Popov's. He was standing in the middle of the pitch, dressed in a navy blue suit and with a cordless microphone in his hand.

'There is nothing to be alarmed about,' he said. 'Please do not run.'

Some of the players were still on the pitch, standing in small groups near the home goal. Orderlies in fluorescent jackets were roaming around Popov. By the dugouts, Jake saw his dad being watched closely by two security guards. He had to get closer to him.

'Dad . . .' he murmured. Jake slipped into one of the rows

of seats and climbed over the top to the row below. It was quicker than using the main aisles, which were packed with people rushing the other way. He found he could balance on the backrest of each seat and step down that way. There was still smoke rising from the wreckage of the VIP box, which had been blown apart. Jake could see the insides of the room exposed – black and charred.

He looked to the dugout again, but there was something wrong. The guards were *too* close to his dad. One of them shoved him in the back, and he could see his dad's body language change.

Jake caught a glint of metal in the security guard's hand.

A gun!

Jake watched in horror as his dad nodded, and made his way into the passage behind the dugout. The security guards followed closely behind and he remembered Truman's order to 'relieve' Jake's dad of his position . . .

Jake bounded over the remaining rows, and vaulted over the advertising hoardings on to the pitch. One of the brightly-dressed groundsmen shouted something, but he didn't hear and sprinted across the turf. Popov was being led off the pitch as well, his back to Jake.

Jake reached the dugout and plunged inside, up the tunnel and past the dressing rooms. He saw his dad being pushed into a lift. As the three men turned, Jake pulled back, catching his breath, willing his heart to slow down just a bit before it exploded in his chest. He heard the lift doors close and thought it safe to come out. The display beside the CALL button read *1* then *2*, counting off the floors.

They're taking him up to Popov's office. To Truman.

Jake thought fast. He couldn't go straight up after them. They'd only kill his dad, then him. No, he had to do something unexpected. There was only one other way to Popov's office, and Jake knew it well.

I had to climb down last time. Now it's time to climb up.

At the back of the stands, he found the spot directly beneath Popov's over-hanging office. It looked more daunting this way: a straight climb twenty metres up. Jake rubbed his hands together and started to climb up on the massive bolts and rivets. It was just like the climbing wall at school – except here Jake would die if he fell. But then he reached the point where the A-frame joined the outer wall of the stadium.

You can do it, he told himself.

Jake wrapped one hand round the bottom of the stanchion, then the other. He heaved himself up, and managed to wrap his legs round the metal. Then he inched up, using his legs to push him along and his arms to keep his upper body against the steel support.

By the time he reached the top of the stanchion his arms were trembling with the effort. He didn't know if he'd have it in him to do the last, tricky part. The office floor was now directly above his head and the lip of the outer sill was two feet away, hidden from view. Jake was grateful at least that this part of the ground was in shadow – no one would see him from the great expanse of the pitch below. Jake let go with one hand, tightened his grip with his legs, and felt for the handhold on the outer wall of the office. He found it – the windowsill.

Now or never! he thought.

He locked the fingers of his right hand over the lip and let go of the stanchion with his left. Scrambling, he managed to get that one in place too, so he had both hands gripping the window ledge, and his legs still wrapped around the stanchion.

He released his legs to swing free below.

One last pull!

Breathing heavily, Jake dragged himself up on to the ledge, straining every last muscle in his arms. He gripped the edges of the outer wall until his knuckles were white, trying to catch his breath. Already he could hear voices from inside. The glass was still cracked from the wayward bullet.

Jake edged along the sill to the glass and peered inside.

His dad was standing in the corner of the room with his hands cuffed behind his back. One of the security guards was pointing a gun at him. The other was seated on the corner of the desk, with his back to Jake.

'What the hell is going on?' his dad said. 'Why's this idiot pointing a gun at me?' Jake couldn't tell who he was speaking to at first, but then Christian Truman stepped into view. He must have been in the small bathroom, because he was holding a bloodied white towel to the side of his head. He'd taken off his jacket and was wearing a white shirt. He walked up to Jake's dad, drew back his fist and punched him in the stomach. Jake flinched at the brutal blow, but kept a firm grip on the ledge. He watched as his dad fell to his knees.

'Don't play innocent with me, Bastin,' Truman said. 'We both know exactly what's going on here.'

Jake's dad caught his breath and looked up. There was anger in his face, but confusion too.

'What are you talking about, Christian? One moment I'm coaching the team, the next I'm being assaulted.'

Truman threw the towel angrily at the glass, and Jake drew back instinctively.

'Cut the crap. You and your son just couldn't keep your noses clean, and I can't have people sniffing around my business.' He went forward again and Jake thought he was going to kick his dad. Instead, he knelt in front of him and seized his jaw between his fingers and thumb. He pulled his face round so they were looking each other in the eye. 'Do you really think I'm that damn stupid?'

Something changed in Jake's dad's face. The mask dropped and he smiled. A hopeless smile.

'Yes, I do.'

Truman backed away and snatched the gun from his bodyguard, then walked forward and pushed the barrel against Jake's dad's cheek. Truman's face was red with rage and his hand was shaking. He stayed in the same position for several seconds, his finger tight against the trigger. Jake held his breath, waiting for the right moment. Then Truman pulled away.

'I hope you die better than your son did,' he sneered.

His dad looked up, eyes flashing with fury and grief, then launched himself at Truman, teeth gnashing. 'You bastard! I'll kill you . . .'

Truman backed off nervously as the guards caught Jake's dad and restrained him. Truman swung the butt of the gun into Jake's dad's temple, opening a cut that bled freely over his eyebrow and cheek. He fell against the edge of the desk on to his knees, and lay on the floor.

Truman handed the gun back to the bodyguard, and walked to the door. 'Don't use the gun,' he said. 'We'll make it look like he died in the stampede.'

He opened the door and left.

Jake watched as his dad struggled to his feet and backed into the wall behind him. One of the bodyguards slipped a knuckleduster over his hand, the second pulled out a foot-long cosh.

Jake's anger swelled. He wasn't going to watch his dad beaten to death by thugs. There was a steel pipe along the top of the window, part of the structure keeping it suspended in the air. Jake grabbed it, then pushed with his feet off the window, swinging backward. The bodyguards turned.

As he swung forward, he kicked as hard as he could in the centre of the pane where the bullet was embedded. Jake prayed the panel was weakened enough.

The glass gave way, splintering from the centre, and crashed across the desk, shattering into hundreds of shards. Jake landed beside the desk. His dad's face rearranged itself in astonishment.

'Jake!'

The guard with the cosh came at Jake first, swinging downward at his head. Jake skipped back, and before the thug could deliver another blow, sent a right cross into his nose. He heard the bone crunch and blood sprayed across the man's cheek. Jake followed in and drove an upper cut with his left hand under the chin. The guard collapsed across the desk chair. He didn't get up.

The second guard came more slowly, in a southpaw stance, the knuckleduster on his front hand. Jake ducked under a jab and came in close for a body blow. His fist bounced harmlessly off, his wrist jarring painfully. The thug smiled.

He's wearing some kind of body armour, Jake realised.

'Hey!' said a voice. The thug turned and saw Jake's dad right behind him. His dad's hands were still cuffed, but he slammed his forehead into the guard's face. The guard fell like a puppet whose strings had been cut.

'Get these cuffs off me,' said Jake's dad, eyes roving his surroundings as if another attack was imminent.

Jake found the keys in the fallen guard's back pocket and unlocked the handcuffs. His dad rubbed his wrists and nodded to the two fallen assailants.

'That was a stupid thing you did,' he said to Jake. 'You could have been killed.'

'You're welcome,' said Jake.

His dad grabbed Jake's arm and pulled him close. 'I'd never have forgiven myself if anything had happened to you. When that bomb went off, I . . .'

Jake pulled way. 'The AEB are safe. I got them out. But listen, it's Devon. He planted the bomb.'

'Hold up,' his dad said. 'Slow down, Jake. Are you telling me that Devon Taylor is an assassin? That's crazy!'

'Dad, he's Truman's *son*!'

Jake explained what had happened after the game started. When he had finished, his dad looked resolute.

'We need to stop them before they escape,' his dad said.

'But they'll be gone already,' said Jake.

'No they won't. Christian Truman wouldn't go by car — he'll keep up appearances, and leave in style.'

Jake pricked his ears and heard a sound — the *thud-thud-thud* of rotor blades. Out of the broken window, a blue and red helicopter hovered over the stadium, angling slowly downward.

'We need to get to the roof,' said Jake. 'Now!'

21

Jake's dad pressed the *R* button in the lift. 'Stay close to me', he said.

'Do you really think he'll run away when he realises the AEB scientists are still alive?' Jake asked.

'I've dealt with men like Truman for years,' his dad said. 'They always get out when it gets hot. Leave the little people to do the dirty work.'

The doors opened on to a deserted lounge, with a marble-topped bar at the far end and tasteful, expensive furnishings spread throughout. Classical music, strangely out of place given the chaos below, tinkled from speakers that Jake couldn't see.

Double doors on the right wall led to a restaurant, and Jake saw several large, circular tables laid out for service. There were four other doors. Two for staff, one for the toilets, and a final one, the nearest, which read 'HELIPAD'.

The door to the toilet suddenly opened and Devon Taylor emerged. He froze when he saw Jake and his dad.

'Thought you could fly away?' asked Jake.

Devon's hands scrambled at his pockets, but whatever he was looking for obviously wasn't there. His eyes went to the helipad exit door, but Jake's dad was closer and blocked off the route. Devon ran instead towards the restaurant, plunging through the double doors. Jake went after him.

'You find Truman!' he shouted to his dad.

The doors to the restaurant were still swinging closed as Jake reached them. He went through and ducked as a wine bottle came spinning through the air, smashing against the doorframe and showering Jake with red wine and glass.

Devon was standing behind a table, wielding a second bottle.

'You're quick,' he sneered. 'For a *kid*.'

Jake dodged the second bottle more easily and it shattered on the floor around the pristine dinner tables.

'I trusted you,' said Jake, moving into the room. 'But you're just a murderer.'

'Maybe,' said Devon. He was backing off, a steak knife in his hand. 'But I'll be a rich one.'

'The richest man in prison,' said Jake, threading between

the tables. There wasn't much room to manoeuvre. He picked up a knife of his own.

Somewhere a gunshot went off, and both Jake and Devon jumped. Two seconds later, he heard a second bullet.

'Sounds like the coach's contract has been terminated,' Devon said.

Jake tried to still his pounding heart and force down the bile that wanted to heave out of him. He shook his head clear of flickering images of his father on the ground, wounded . . . *bleeding* . . .

'The AEB escaped, you know,' he said to Devon. 'The plan failed.'

Devon clenched his jaw. 'Nice try . . .'

'It's the truth,' said Jake. 'They got out just in time. I made sure of it.'

'Then you've signed your own death warrant,' Devon said, jumping up on to one of the tables, lithe as a cat. Jake climbed on to one too, knocking aside several wine glasses.

Devon hopped on to a nearer table. Now there was just one between them.

'Let's see what you've got, Bastin,' Devon said.

At the same moment, they leapt on to the table separating them. Jake thrust with his knife, but missed, and Devon swung his in a wide arc. Jake tried to dodge, but felt a stinging pain across his stomach. He cried out and looked down. Blood seeped through his T-shirt.

'There's no one to sub in now,' Devon said.

Jake's rage took over and he charged. He hit Devon in a high rugby tackle and they both fell from the table and slammed into the floor among the chairs. Jake heard Devon's knife clatter against something as it flew out of the player's grasp. Jake got his hands on Devon's throat and began to squeeze. Devon struggled, trying to reach Jake's own throat but Jake tucked his chin into his neck, pressing his legs tight to Devon's waist.

Jake clenched with all his strength as Devon started choking. Devon's face was going purple. In his rage, Jake realised what he was capable of. He would not stop until he'd choked the life out of Devon Taylor.

Suddenly the chair seat beside Jake's head exploded and stuffing flew out. A split second later he heard another gunshot. Truman twenty feet away was aiming his gun at Jake's head. He rolled off Devon and under the table as another shot splintered a glass.

Beneath the table, concealed by the overhanging tablecloth, it was like being in a cave. But Jake knew he couldn't stay there long.

'Pop, he's under here!' spluttered Devon.

Jake squeezed between two chairs on his hands and knees and crawled under the next table.

'Where is he?' shouted Christian Truman.

'I don't know,' whined Devon. 'He's here somewhere. What happened to the coach?'

'I dealt with him,' said Truman. 'You hear that, kid?' he shouted. 'There are some shots even the legendary Steve Bastin can't defend against.'

My dad's dead.

An angry sob escaped Jake's lips.

I'll kill you, you bastard. I promise.

He moved under the next table. Another gunshot went off, thudding into a surface nearby. He had to find a way to get the advantage back.

'I saw the cloth move,' said Truman. 'Where are you, you little rat?'

The restaurant was silent apart from the sounds of Truman and Devon moving about.

Jake tried to keep his breathing steady.

He peered under the hem of the cloth, and saw a door. He'd lost his bearings a bit, but he guessed it was the restaurant kitchen. If he could get inside, maybe he could find a weapon. Redress the balance there.

The door was ten feet away.

Please be open!

'You know this ends badly for you,' said Devon. 'Let's get it over with quickly. It won't hurt.'

You're going to be the one hurting, Jake promised silently. He lifted the cloth gently and readied himself to run.

'Devon's right,' said Truman. 'But listen, maybe we can talk about this. Man to man.'

Right! thought Jake. *You shot my dad, and now you're just going to let me go?*

He heard a whisper, but couldn't make out what was said. He guessed father and son were signalling to each other, pointing as they fanned across the room.

Jake stood up and ran towards the door.

'Get him!' Devon shouted. A shot went off as Jake threw himself against the door. It was more flimsy than it looked and opened easily on smooth hinges. Jake fell through and landed on his front on the floor. He quickly scrambled up and took in the room. A commercial kitchen, around four times the size of the one at Obed in London. All stainless steel and chrome. Three aisles. Cooking implements hung from hooks and pans of all sizes lined the shelves. At the far end were several ovens, and what looked like walk-in fridges and freezers. There was a fire exit at the back.

I have to create a distraction.

Jake ran first to the dishwasher and pulled down the side panel, hitting a green switch. It began to operate with a swishing noise. Then he switched on open grills and burners. He twisted an egg timer, which ticked quietly as it counted down.

Jake heard the door open and ducked behind a deep fat fryer. He turned the dial and it started up with a hum.

'We know you're in here,' said Truman. 'Stop running, Jake.'

The kitchen was awash with noise.

Jake stayed close to the cold floor. On a low shelf was a pile of strainers and colanders. He picked one out and hurled it down the aisle. It clattered to the far end.

'Got him!' Devon said. Jake heard Truman and Devon's steps as they went to investigate. He ran, crouching, the length of the second aisle, and saw a carving knife lying across a chopping board. He snatched it up and hid behind a tall cabinet containing baking trays and roasting tins.

He was back near the door to the restaurant.

I might be able to make it.

Then Truman walked into view a few feet away. Jake saw the gun first, held in Truman's outstretched arm. He wouldn't get a better chance.

Jake jumped out and slashed the knife across Truman's hand. The American roared and dropped the gun. Jake heard it clatter somewhere in the room, but didn't see where. He turned to face Truman with the knife, as the Texan gripped his injured hand. Jake pressed the knife up against his throat, and found tears were welling in his eyes. 'You killed my dad, you −'

'Nice try, Jake,' said a voice behind.

Devon had picked up the gun.

'Shoot the little wretch,' snarled Truman. 'He's starting to get on my nerves.'

'My pleasure,' said Devon, raising the barrel. 'Final whistle, Bastin.'

Jake closed his eyes, but the screech of leather on the linoleum floor made him open them again. A flash of silver came from nowhere and crashed into Devon's head. He dropped the gun and cried out as a baking tray rattled to the floor beside him. Jake launched himself forward and drove a foot into Truman's chest, sending him crashing backward over a work surface.

Another figure staggered out. Pale, and holding a hand to his bloodied shoulder, it was Jake's dad.

'You!' said Truman.

'Just about,' his dad said. There was another hole in his shirt, black at the edges, over his heart. He knocked on his chest. 'Not exactly part of the kit, but Kevlar comes in handy sometimes.'

218

Devon was reaching for the gun on the floor but Jake got there first and kicked it across to his dad, who picked it up and pointed it straight at Devon.

'Game over, Taylor. Why don't you join your "pop"?'

Christian Truman was still nursing his hand, while Jake opened the huge fridge door. His dad motioned the two men inside.

'In there?' snarled Devon. 'We'll freeze to death.'

Jake's dad's face hardened. 'It's kept at four degrees above freezing. It'll cool you down while the authorities make their way here.'

Truman glared at Jake with pure hatred. 'You'll pay for this,' he said. 'And don't think I'm going to any jail – my lawyers could make *Hitler* look innocent of all charges. I'll be seeing you two again. Bank on that.'

Jake's dad swung the door closed and they used a mop handle to prevent the lever mechanism being opened from inside.

'Will they really be OK?' asked Jake.

'Hypothermia won't even set in for an hour. Our guys will be here before that.' He pulled out his phone and dialled a single number, waited, then entered a four-digit code.

'Hi, this is Bastin. I need a clean-up at the stadium

restaurant and kitchen . . . that's right. Truman and Devon Taylor are on ice. Take them into custody. I'll debrief at HQ.' He closed the phone.

'Aren't we going to wait for the police?' Jake asked.

'Negative. We were never even here.' His dad winced and touched his shoulder.

'What about that?' said Jake. 'You've been shot. We need to get you to a hospital.'

'I know a place in St Petersburg,' his dad said. 'We'll go there.'

With a jacket covering his injury, they took a taxi to a clinic in the middle of the city. Jake was surprised that his dad greeted the man at the front desk in English, and was shown through to a back room. A female doctor came through. She eyed Jake with suspicion, but smiled at his dad.

'Just a patch, please, Sarah. This is my son, Jake, by the way.'

'Hello, Steve,' she said. 'Good to see you again. And nice to meet you too, Jake. I'm Dr Young.'

Jake nodded hello.

Another of my dad's contacts? Just like Lester. They're everywhere.

The doctor peeled back the Tigers shirt that Jake's dad

had placed over the wound, and sucked in a deep breath. 'What's this then? A thirty-two?'

'God, you're good,' his dad said, grinning. 'On the paper-work, let's just say I fell down the stairs.'

'You got it.'

Dr Young and his dad spoke like old friends as she cleaned the wound, added stitches and then placed a dressing over the top. Apparently the bullet had passed clean through. They left, less than an hour later, with his dad's arm in a sling and strict instructions to change the bandages daily.

Jake was shattered by the time they arrived back at the house, the day's events suddenly overtaking him. His dad looked ready to drop, too.

'We'll talk in the morning, yes?' his dad said.

'Sure,' replied Jake.

'And, Jake,' said his dad.

'Hm?'

'You made me really proud today.'

'Thanks, Dad.'

22

His dad was already in the kitchen when Jake woke up the next day.

'Want some eggs?' his dad asked. He'd loosened his sling and was holding a pan with his injured arm.

Just like old times.

'I'll do that,' said Jake, taking it from him.

His dad sat down at the table, scanning a newspaper. The lead article showed a picture of the chaos at the stadium, with the headline: *Accident or Terrorists?*

As Jake grilled bread, and cracked eggs into a dish, his dad spoke. 'You know you can't tell anyone about this, don't you? Not even Mum.'

Jake whisked the eggs with a fork. 'What? Or you'd have to kill me?'

His dad didn't smile. 'I need you to be serious. My identity: it's a state secret. If it ever got out, we'd all be in danger. Mum included.'

Jake put the pan on the hob. 'I understand. Just tell me one thing. Was this . . . this job . . . was it the reason you two got divorced?'

Jake's dad sighed. 'Your mum never knew. So, in a way, I guess it might have been. Secrets are not good for any relationship.'

I know all about that.

There was a knock on the door.

'Must be Karenya,' Jake said.

He opened the door, and standing there was Popov. Jake stepped back involuntarily.

Popov's face broke into a grin. 'Well, Jake, aren't you going to invite an old friend in?'

Jake recovered. 'Sure, sorry, come in.' For some reason, Jake was reminded of that rule in vampire stories: never *invite* one into your home.

Popov stepped inside. To Jake's surprise he didn't have a bodyguard with him.

Jake's dad was standing up now. 'Good morning, Igor. This is unexpected.'

'I thought I'd come by and see how you both were after yesterday's unfortunate events. You have hurt your arm, I see?'

'It's nothing,' Jake's dad said. 'Just a sprained elbow.'

'Well, you should let my private doctor take a look,' Popov said.

'It's quite all right,' Jake's dad replied.

Jake looked from his dad to the Russian. There was some kind of electricity in the air, like just before a lightning storm. So what if Popov hadn't been involved in *this* plan to kill the scientists? Was that just because Truman had thought of it first?

Jake scanned the room for a weapon. Nothing.

A smell of burning reached his nose.

'The eggs!' his dad exclaimed.

He went quickly to the pan and took it off the hob. As he did, Jake saw him scoop a knife off the side. His dad turned back to face Popov, concealing the knife behind his back.

This doesn't look good.

'I'm sorry to interrupt your breakfast,' said Popov. 'I came to deliver some sad news.'

'Oh, yes?' said Jake's dad.

Jake began to panic. Had the AEB been killed after all?

'Yes,' said Popov, inspecting his cufflinks. 'I'm afraid that both Christian Truman and Devon Taylor were killed yesterday at the football ground.' Jake looked at his dad in alarm as Popov continued. 'It seems that after he was taken off the field, Devon joined his fellow countryman in the VIP box. We had thought everyone had escaped, but two corpses were discovered in the wreckage late last night.'

'It can't be,' said Jake.

Popov raised an eyebrow. 'I assure you,' he said coldly, 'it is *definitely* them.'

A glance from his dad told Jake to drop it.

'A terrible loss,' said Popov, 'but the cloud has a silver edge, as you say in the West.'

'Igor,' said Jake's dad, 'Devon was one of the most promising players of his generation. He was an inspiration to countless children around the world. He . . .'

'He made a mistake,' interrupted Popov, glaring at Jake. The ice in his reptile–eyes made Jake's skin prickle. What did he mean, a mistake? Did Popov know that Truman was planning to frame him? 'If it hadn't been for his rash actions, he would still be alive.'

Jake swallowed, but managed to nod. 'You're right. It was a bad tackle.'

Popov smiled, with little warmth.

'You mentioned a silver lining,' said Jake's dad.

'Oh, yes,' said Popov, brightening suddenly. 'In light of Mr Truman's sudden *departure*, and his lack of immediate kin, one of my own subsidiaries has taken over as the major shareholder in Truman Energy. It means that we can still pursue the alternative energy research that will surely be Russia's – indeed the world's – future.'

'That's great news, Igor,' said Jake's dad. 'And the AEB? Will that continue?'

'I'm afraid that all three of the scientists have decided to take their expertise back to their native countries for the time being,' said Popov. 'You can imagine that recent events have somewhat shaken their confidence. We will find others to replace them, I'm sure.'

'I'm sure,' repeated Jake's dad. 'Is there anything else we can do for you?'

Popov took a few steps forward until he was only a foot away from Jake's dad. Jake saw his dad's fingers tighten around the knife's hilt, and tried not to stare at it too openly. If Popov was aware of any danger, he didn't show it.

Popov sighed. 'I'm sorry to say that our little experiment with the Tigers must come to an end. It will take some time to restore the stadium, and even longer to repair the damage to my reputation. The culprits must be identified and prosecuted. No one crosses Igor Popov. *No one.* You understand?'

The threat hung in the air.

'Of course,' Jake's dad said. 'People must be reassured that such an event could never happen again.'

'Exactly!' exclaimed Popov, looking suddenly pleased with himself. He walked quickly towards the open door. 'I will of course honour the financial aspects of your contract. I am, after all, a respectable man.'

'Thank you,' said Jake's dad. 'It's been a pleasure working with you.'

'I'm sure our paths will cross again.' Popov flashed a smile. 'And farewell to you too, Jake Bastin. I hope we meet again.'

He stared at Jake, unblinking, then closed the door behind him silently. As Popov's car skidded away across the gravel drive, Jake turned angrily to his dad.

'So that's what you meant by "clean up"! Cold-blooded murder?'

'Jake,' his dad said, 'it wasn't us. I swear. MI6 should have taken them in for interrogation. Our government doesn't kill prisoners.'

'Well, it seems like there are two corpses who'd beg to differ.'

'Wait, Jake, just give me a minute.'

While Jake emptied the burnt eggs into the bin and made a cup of coffee, his dad dialled his contact and asked what was going on. He listened for several seconds, nodding and rubbing his temple. Every so often he punctuated the conversation with a concise question or comment. 'You're sure? . . . Well, what do they know? . . . No, the contract's terminated . . .'

After a few minutes, he hung up.

'Well?' said Jake.

'I'm afraid it's true,' his dad said. 'Our crew got to the kitchens but Truman and Taylor were already gone. The fire crew found them both, side by side, in the stands beneath the VIP box. Looks like Popov's guys got there first.'

Jake imagined Popov's men taking Truman and his son to the VIP box − the scene of their treachery − and throwing them off. Russian justice.

'Popov's an animal,' said Jake.

'I know. But it's best not to think about it,' his dad said.

'What do you mean? We need to go after him. He's a murderer . . .'

'He's just another criminal,' said his dad. 'There are people like Popov all over the world. We can only take down one at a time. The Trumans have been stopped. The AEB are safe.'

'So Popov gets away with it,' said Jake, exasperated.

'Not forever. He'll slip up sometime.'

Jake slammed a hand on to the counter top. 'Damn it!' he cursed.

Somehow the Russian had ended up in a better position

than he started in. More money, more opportunities, and somehow blameless.

'Jake, don't let this get personal,' his dad said.

'How can you say that?' asked Jake. 'After what happened to Chernoff? He was your friend, wasn't he?'

'He was,' his dad said grimly. 'He said he had something to tell me that night in the restaurant. He never got the chance. I assumed it was Popov . . .'

'But now you think he was going to warn you about Truman?' Jake asked.

'I guess we'll never know.'

Jake could almost see his dad's emotions shifting inside him. Slow and steady, as always.

The taxi was booked for later that afternoon and Jake had one last swim in the pool to clear his thoughts. His body was a mess of cuts and bruises. A week in Russia left him looking like he'd been in a war zone.

He was completing a final length when his dad entered.

'Jake,' he said, his tone ominous in the echoing poolroom, 'can I have a word?'

Jake pulled up to the side and rested with both elbows on the marble floor. He wiped the hair back out of his eyes.

'Sure. What is it?'

His dad sat down heavily on a wicker chair.

'How would you feel about not going straight back to London?'

'What do you mean?' Jake asked.

'Well, a little thing's come up. Another job, in Italy.'

'A *job*?'

His dad grinned. 'Sky are short of a pundit for the international tournament. There's a plane heading to Milan tonight.'

'Just a studio sofa, then?' said Jake, smiling back.

His dad shrugged. 'That's all I'm saying.'

'You know,' Jake said, 'you used to be a better liar.'

His dad stood up and walked to the edge of the pool.

'I spoke to Central Command last night,' he said. 'They are not all happy with it, but I assured them you had a good head on you, and could be trusted. They'll want to meet you properly at some point, but they saw no harm in letting you tag along. If anything, it helps my cover. Dad with son in tow, y'know?'

Jake thought about what his dad was saying. He was standing on the threshold of a new life. One of secrets. Of danger. There could be no going back once the threshold was crossed.

'A team?' Jake said.

'As long as I'm the coach,' his dad replied. 'What d'ya say?'

Jake pushed off from the side with his feet and drifted towards the centre of the pool, where he stopped.

You can be the coach, he thought, *but I'll be the star striker!*

'I'm in,' Jake said.

COMING IN SEPTEMBER 2010

Jake Bastin is in Milan for an international football tournament.
His dad will be the TV commentator – but Jake suspects this is a
front. He is sure his dad's there on covert business.
If only Jake could get close to the action . . .

Instead he is stuck at a photo shoot for a priceless South African
diamond. Then a massive diamond heist takes place . . .
Brutal assassinations follow. And Jake finds himself playing
centre forward in another international scandal.

But this time, it's personal.

EGMONT PRESS: ETHICAL PUBLISHING

Egmont Press is about turning writers into successful authors and children into passionate readers – producing books that enrich and entertain. As a responsible children's publisher, we go even further, considering the world in which our consumers are growing up.

Safety First
Naturally, all of our books meet legal safety requirements. But we go further than this; every book with play value is tested to the highest standards – if it fails, it's back to the drawing-board.

Made Fairly
We are working to ensure that the workers involved in our supply chain – the people that make our books – are treated with fairness and respect.

Responsible Forestry
We are committed to ensuring all our papers come from environmentally and socially responsible forest sources.

For more information, please visit our website at www.egmont.co.uk/ethical

Egmont is passionate about helping to preserve the world's remaining ancient forests. We only use paper from legal and sustainable forest sources, so we know where every single tree comes from that goes into every paper that makes up every book.

This book is made from paper certified by the Forestry Stewardship Council (FSC), an organisation dedicated to promoting responsible management of forest resources. For more information on the FSC, please visit **www.fsc.org**. To learn more about Egmont's sustainable paper policy, please visit **www.egmont.co.uk/ethical**.